From The Won
34 Great Sutton S

Lisa Greenwood was born in 1955 and began writing in 1983. This is her first novel. She lives in Aukland, New Zealand, with her daughter.

Lisa Greenwood

The Roundness of Eggs

The Women's Press

First published in Great Britain by The Women's Press 1988
A member of the Namara Group
34 Great Sutton Street, London EC1V 0DX

First published by Benton Ross Publishers Ltd,
46 Parkway Drive, Glenfield, Auckland 10, New Zealand

British Library Cataloguing in Publication Data

Greenwood, Lisa
The roundness of eggs.
I. Title
823[F]

ISBN 0-7043-4140-9

Reproduced, printed and bound in Great Britain by
Hazell Watson & Viney Limited,
Member of the BPCC Group,
Aylesbury, Bucks

CHAPTER ONE

A BLACKBIRD FALLS to the ground in the garden. For some days Olive watches it scurry in the borders and flutter beneath hydrangea bushes. It looks healthy enough. A lustre plays over the dark plumage and its eye is sharp but the bird appears to be incapable of flight.

Another blackbird stays close. Its flight cuts an arc backwards and forwards across the lawn and up into the trees. Jumping anxiously from branch to branch it will hurtle into the air once more, swooping down low over the grass and turning at the last moment to glide up into the welcoming branches of apple or plum.

The grounded partner makes no move to join it in the air.

Fly up, Olive thinks. Fly up. Lift up and away. This chant sounds over and over in her head.

Nothing happens. It makes her feel nervous. With one finger she traces the blue edging on her plate. It is a line consistent all the way around. Pushing toast crusts from one side to the other she directs them into patterns. Each way she arranges them, the shapes they make are square or angular.

She calls to Jim. 'Have you heard the fuss in the garden?'

His electric razor starts up in the bathroom. 'I can't hear you,' he says.

Taking the crusts she breaks them in half and makes a new design. This time they are diagonal lines running the same way, like rain.

The noise of the razor stops and she calls out again. 'Have you heard the fuss in the garden?'

'What fuss?'

'Two blackbirds out there. One's injured or something and the other one's trying to protect it. It goes crazy when I go out into the garden.'

Jim appears at the doorway with the razor in one hand. He blows into it and a thin cloud of whiskers shoot out. For a moment they float, then slowly drift down to speckle the floor. Some are still black but most are grey.

'A cat will get it,' he says.

And so on this early Wednesday morning a sentence is passed.

Olive enters the bedroom and pulls her nightdress up over her head. Dropping it on the bed she wanders around the room. Carpet springs beneath her feet. The pile is full.

Another day, she thinks. Ahh it is a blank. Nothing shows through the mist ahead.

Jim comes in behind. 'You're getting goose-pimples on your legs.'

'I don't know what to wear.'

'Jesus, Olive, you've lost weight. Look at those ribs sticking up in your chest. Look how bony your chest is.' Startled, he looks up.

'I know.'

'Why have you lost so much weight?'

'I don't know.'

'What do you mean, you don't know?'

'I suppose I'm getting old.'

'Age has absolutely nothing to do with it.'

'No.'

'Besides, fifty-one is hardly old.'

'Fifty-two.'

'You look like a chook all around here.' He prods at his own collarbones with a stiff finger.

'A chook?'

'A hen.'

'A Rhode Island red?'

'I don't know. Any sort I suppose.'

'That's flattering.'

'I thought you liked chooks.'

Jim brushes his suit jacket at the mirror. A tall man, he bends at the knee and leans back to see his reflection.

One hand runs down over his sleeve.

Olive watches. At fifty-eight he is still young. Despite his being six years older and grey where she is still dark, she appears the elder. Lately there has been a change in her skin and eyes. It is a dulling. There is no spark.

Wearily she shuts her eyes and an image of astonishing clarity springs before her. It is an egg. A massive egg whose shell is bluish and faintly speckled.

Half-shadowed, it turns through deepest space. Pinprick stars glitter in the background. The sound it makes is a hush.

Alarmed, Olive's eyes jerk open. An egg in space. The perfect egg. What does it mean?

'There's a sea bird,' she says in a rush. 'That lays its eggs on cliff ledges and the egg is pear-shaped so if it gets knocked out of the nest it rolls around in a circle back to where it started from. Safe from the yawning abyss below.'

'Safe from what?'

'The yawning abyss below.'

'Here in New Zealand?'

'I don't know. Overseas, I think. I read it somewhere. Those words stuck in my mind.'

'Which words?'

'The yawning abyss below.'

'Oh.'

Jim turns back to the mirror. His hand is smooth on the wooden handle of the clothes-brush.

'When I was a child,' Olive blurts out, 'my brother and I used to eat blackbird eggs. And thrushes'.'

Jim stops brushing and turns. 'You can't do that. You can't eat blackbird eggs.'

'We did. Father sent us out on the farm in the mornings with a little bag to put them in.'

'You actually ate them?'

'They're just eggs.'

'They'd be full of germs.'

'Why would an egg have germs?'

'Birds have all sorts of diseases.'

'But eggs don't.'

'I wouldn't be so sure.'

'We were poor. We used to try and fill the whole little bag. I think that was about a dozen eggs but sometimes they had baby birds in them and we couldn't eat those ones.'

'That's disgusting.'

'Mostly we had them scrambled.'

'Jesus.'

'It was a grey felt bag and it had "William" embroidered on it with orange thread and a border of little orange bumps. And a drawstring at the top. It was supposed to be for marbles but he didn't have any anyway.'

Olive is crying. Tears slide down her face and her shoulders shake. Disorderly sobs break from her throat into the quiet of this early mid-week morning.

Abruptly she sits down on the bed.

'Love, come on now. What's going on?'

At hearing tenderness in Jim's voice she cries even more. She is unable to answer.

'Put something on,' he says. 'Look, you'll freeze.'

Reaching for the nightdress she pushes her arms into the sleeves and pulls it back over her head. She wipes the hem over her face then smooths the garment on her knees.

Jim is just standing there watching. He glances at his watch. 'I'll have to leave for work in a minute. I'm late already. You'll be all right?'

'Yes, of course.'

Olive is overcome with longing for comfort. Hold me or I'll drown. She yearns for nothing more than to collapse into his arms this very minute. To smell the wool of his jacket and feel it dry on her cheek.

Her thoughts are slow and confused. Hold me or I'll drown. It is a child's voice and insistent. Don't think such things. She moves from it, piling blocks in the way until the voice is gone. Her legs swing on the side of the bed.

'Stop doing that,' Jim says.

Her feet are grinding into the carpet. The underlay is spongy below.

'What's it like living in the same house you grew up in?' she says.

'You're always asking that.'

'What did the house feel like when you were a child?'

He packs the papers and books into his briefcase. He holds a brochure up and his eyes skim the cover. 'I don't know what you mean.'

Brushing her face with the back of one hand Olive can taste the salt in her mouth. 'Do you love me?' she asks.

'This isn't like you.'

'But do you?'

'Of course I do.'

'I'm sorry.'

'That's better now.'

'I'll get organised.'

'Good girl. You're okay.' Tapping her bottom with a rolled-up newspaper he hurries past.

Kissing him goodbye at the front door Olive smells the cologne on his face. His jaw is sleek.

Spinning away, he bounds down the steps and onto the path. His shoulders are broad from behind. The suit fits perfectly.

'Goodbye!' she cries.

He waves without looking back then his hand is at his side again.

Off he goes, she thinks. Off into the world. Pulling the heavy door closed she moves back inside the house.

The light changes in some way. Olive sits at the table amongst the breakfast dishes. The cloth is gritty with crumbs and cold coffee rests at the bottom of a mug.

Who can tell how much time passes. Rain falls lightly on the window. Dry glass still shows between the specks but the area diminishes. Now the whole of it is wet.

Taking up the morning newspaper Olive glances at the headlines. They blur from words to black marks and back to words again but there is no interest. She puts the paper aside and pushes her chair back.

Opening the back door she moves out onto the steps. Sitting on the top step Olive watches the rain. A blackbird screeches in the boughs of the rimu. Beneath the tree there is a dry space where the lower branches almost sweep the ground. She watches the dark space.

Shelter there, shelter there. The trunk is strong for support and the canopy impenetrable overhead. In her mind the flightless bird is safe beneath the tree. Nothing moves.

Drops of water splash from leaf to leaf in the camellia and big drops hang suspended on the clothes-line. They are a string of milky beads.

Although close to the centre of Auckland the garden is a large expanse of green. The neighbouring houses are screened by vegetation. The tall trees down one side and along the bottom boundary are sixty years old. The orchard is more recent but not so young as to be without a maturity of its own. Grey lichen drapes from the trunk and spreading boughs of the plum.

The voiceless rain falls. The blackbird's call has stopped and the ensuing silence is ominous. A cold current moves in Olive's chest. The ice which is fear sweeps up from below.

'Sing out!' she cries, but the bird is quite still.

There is no flutter in the weeping foliage to indicate a place. Water drips from each trailing strand.

Olive looks away but it is to something else now. A bareness stands out at the bottom of the garden. A pale colour shows where there should be nothing but the green.

She turns to one side but the pull is too much and her eyes are swinging back.

The avocado tree is dying. It leans at a strange angle in a litter of leaves and those still on the branches are discoloured.

Her hands are up over her mouth. That she hadn't noticed any change! The lawn in the orchard is brown with fallen leaves. Each one glistens with the wet but the avocado is an evergreen.

Not that there is a total absence of beauty in the circle of fallen leaves around the trunk. They shine yellow on emerald grass like a circle of lights. Or quinces. Or a ring of fallen lemons. But as well as this there is something curiously unpleasant.

The tree is me. The thought causes Olive to gasp as

if she is drowning this very minute. The words and the vision have come from nowhere and will not leave. Her fingers grip the edge of the step she sits upon.

She sees the tree slowly shedding leaves and the bleak form of its branches emerging. And at the same time her own body withers. Barer and whiter the bleached branches become and by the time the tree is quite stark her strength is all but gone.

'They can bury me under the tree,' she mutters and her voice is harsh in the wet quiet.

Jumping to her feet and turning at the same time Olive snaps her eyes shut. What don't I want to see? That which is obvious. She trips and her eyes shoot open and the garden spins upside down as she crashes from step to step.

She stops sprawled on the wet path below. The concrete is cold. In time her head lifts. Rivulets of water open out and fan across. Pain creeps in her legs and her face is pressing down onto the path again and she is turning so now it is her back pressing down. The nightdress is plastered wet across.

Rain falls on her face. The sky is dark grey, almost black. Her lips are apart and the soft rain falls onto her tongue. The water is cold and sweet but it is the salt in her mouth which makes it seem so. When the lingering taste of brine has washed away, the rain is cool and bitter.

Olive takes a box of photographs from a cupboard in the front room. Stepping back she looks around, then bends to put them on the floor. A picture on the top catches her eye.

The four children stand on sand in front of a glittering summer sea. Rising dark and flat behind is the peak of Rangitoto. A solitary cloud hangs above. A scoop of ice cream floats in the bright sky.

Michael is eight years old, Annette is five and the twins are toddlers. Fine blond hair stands out on the tan of the girls' plump arms. Their dresses are red, white and blue. The fabric is patterned with scarlet boats and curving white sails on a background of ultramarine. Buttons down the back are not visible in the picture but they dance up from the depths of Olive's memory. The shapes are fashioned as anchors, each with coiled plastic ropes.

She can see them as clearly as if they are in her hand this very minute. Just thinking of it sets her fingers twitching as though the textured plastic is there to be felt.

For a long time Olive kneels peering through photographs in the dim light. Mainly they are the children in various stages of growth. She looks at them almost without recognition, or is it with an excess of recognition? They are both indelibly familiar and also strangers. Rain strokes its rhythm on the roof.

At the bottom of the box she uncovers a small bundle of old brown photographs. Two rubber bands bind them together and her fingers are working to release them. Without even looking she feels the old sadness swell.

Staring out gully-eyed is her father's face. He stands alone in front of the milking shed. A metal bucket is caught frozen as it swings from his hand. His expression is melancholic.

In the next one — an earlier photograph — her parents stand together with a large grey pumpkin. The vegetable is displayed so the size may be admired. Olive holds her baby brother at their feet. Her eyes squint, although the sun shines from behind and his are open wide.

The photograph has been folded and a white crease runs up the middle, creating two factions. Olive is with her mother and William with their father. The pumpkin is cut cleanly in half.

Olive looks at the girl's small hands in the picture and then examines her own. Looking from the left to the right she turns back again to her left hand. Blue veins run across it below worn skin. The surface is wrinkled in a way it wasn't previously. Is this the same hand? It seems scarcely probable.

How strange to think this child is me! The longer Olive looks the odder it becomes. The smiling girl turns first into a stranger then simply dissolves into a series of black and grey dots. The collection of shapes and shades has no meaning at all.

The other people initially remain clear. Her mother's Irish face is plump and pretty but now that is melting away also.

She was happy then, Olive thinks bitterly. And all these years later her mother's illness rises like bile in her mouth. The years of visiting the hospital and seeing her so fat and strange and getting even stranger. The years of watching her sink back further and further. My mother looking out through different eyes, she thinks. A mother not even knowing her own family any more.

The dark mist of Olive's childhood glides through. There is no part it will not permeate. After a time her feelings of sorrow for her family change to become pity for herself.

Here I am, she thinks. A middle-aged woman crouched on the floor with my head bent down. Crying into my hands. You've got your mother's hands. What does that mean? Who said it? Try to remember as I weep and weep.

Over the Waitemata Harbour thunder rolls. The sound is not deep and rich so much as a low, surly rumble.

If anyone could see me squatting in the corner, a part of Olive's mind is thinking. They would think me crazy too. Crazy like my mother.

The fog rears up again. Clouds swirl across. The shadows are moving in. Little light is able to penetrate. Not much light beaming in. Into this life. These are the things she is thinking.

Many years have passed now since there was a need to grieve. This makes it twice in one day. 'Salt in an old wound,' she mumbles. But what is the salt?

Rising to her feet she moves stiffly across the room. Through the window the street gleams charcoal the same as the sky. A car passes and its tyres leave two ribbons of silver on the seal.

Ahh, Olive thinks. There are no answers to be read out there.

Long slanting lines of rain gently ease the marks away until the street is uniform as before.

In the afternoon the rain eases then stops and Olive hangs the washing in the garden. Taking damp garments from the basket she spreads them with her hands. The cloud cover is low and wet towels and shirts are inanimate on the line. All is dark and still.

Pausing, she looks around. There is a flannel in her hand and she's screwing it up tighter and tighter and now unwinding it. Her grip loosens so the piece of cloth may fall back into the basket.

What is it? The silence is unnerving. The cloud blanket is low and insulating so everything is dark underneath and yet the colours are more intense than usual.

In the shadow of the side wall chrysanthemums bloom. The shades range from red to gold and yellow and white. The white ones stand out. They glow with an absolute purity of colour.

Olive moves across the lawn towards them. Each petal curves in towards the centre of the flower. In the middle they are small and tight but around the outside the petals are larger and less restrained.

A photograph from the morning rises in her vision. The twins as little girls stand hand in hand in a paddock. A clump of arum lilies grows in the foreground and behind the fence the backdrop is dense bush.

Because of the angle the lilies are alabaster against a shade deep as black. The stark flowers are elegant. Olive is moved by some aspect of their simple curving lines.

And now in the garden the white chrysanthemums luminous upon dark green foliage take on an extra beauty. It is almost more than she can bare to look at.

Move away, she thinks, and then she is. Her feet leave marks on the wet lawn. Old hydrangea blooms stand out stiffly on long stalks at the bottom of the wall. They have changed, taking on strange metallic hues. Flowers which were pale blue are now turquoise and the tips are maroon or dry green.

I'll cut them back, Olive thinks, but something is moving beneath the bush. The movement is clear as is the damp rustling sound that it makes.

A cat. It must be a cat. But the movement is too slight and erratic. There is a glimpse of softness and of black. It is the injured bird. Struggling to move, its legs fold under its body and one wing splays to the side.

Desperately Olive looks over her shoulder to the white chrysanthemums. Each perfect bloom is motionless. Their beauty offers no reassurance.

Sickened, she bends down onto her knees and reaches under the bush. Wet leaves kiss her face and she's pulling back. The bird is still now, as if waiting. Her hand inches forward until it touches feathers and her fingers close around.

Lifting it away from the bush she moves back. The bird is warm and light and still in her hand. There is something sticky. Blood. A sinister jewel forms.

Her stomach clenches. Blood has come from a deep puncture in the bird's chest and a crimson drop spreads gleaming on her palm.

Olive stands rigid on the grass. The bird tilts its head one way then the other. The movement is barely perceptible. There is no struggle. Sharp upon its round eye is the distorted reflection of her own face. Turn away from that. Don't look at the moon face and stretched lips.

She is moving up the lawn and unlatching a door at the back of the house. In the old basement laundry she waits for her eyes to adjust. Cobwebs reach right across the washtub. Taking a bucket she half fills it with cold water then adds hot until the temperature is lukewarm.

Without looking at what her hand is doing Olive plunges the bird in. There is just one movement. A flutter breathes against her fingers. There is nothing more. The flashing eye is still. How easily it dies.

Rolling the limp body from one hand to the other she stops. Air holds tight in her lungs. Blood on the palm of her right hand has not come off in the water.

Putting the bird down she pushes both hands into the bucket. Frantically she scrubs at the spot but the stain refuses to lift. It seems etched into her skin. She rubs until her hand stings but the blood is no less intense. I have the mark now, she thinks. The quiet desperation grows.

The garden is silent. There is no sign of the other blackbird. Olive scans the lawn. Her eyes run over the mass of branches in the orchard and back to the trailing bronze green of rimu. There is nothing.

In frigid clay beneath the chrysanthemums she scrapes a shallow grave. The limp body seems smaller now. Wet soil comes down and her hands are pressing it firm.

'Rest in peace,' she whispers, barely hearing the words for the roaring in her ears.

Jumping to her feet she is running blindly for the house. The steps are slippery and leaping from one to the next Olive is almost knocked off her feet by a flock of birds which fly from the house through the open back door.

There appear to be a dozen or more and they are small and sooty although as they pass from the shadow of the house they are for an instant quite silver in colour. Their tails seem split into two feathers like a swallow's. Such is their speed they have gone before she has seen them clearly.

Clinging to the handrail Olive peers into the house. All is still and as usual. And now scanning the empty grey sky it occurs to her that she might have imagined the entire flock.

To imagine such birds. But no, she thinks. For I felt the cool breath of their flight on my cheek. Of that there is no doubt.

She touches her face and it is cold.

'Wake up, wake up.'

From a long distance Olive hears these words. Something pushes her shoulder.

'No, no, not now.' This voice, rough and anguished, is her own. Half awake she pulls herself upright. Night has fallen.

'What's not now? What are you doing in bed?' In the gloom Jim's face is a pale blur.

'What time is it?' she asks.

'Eight o'clock. What are you doing in bed?'

'I don't know.' Pulled from a deep sleep Olive is disorientated. Her heart thumps.

'What's going on?'

'I feel . . . ah . . . so strange. Would you put the light on?'

Thick and yellow the light is not entirely pleasant but

is better than the dark. The big blue vase on the dressing table looks foreign. The unfamiliar light gives it a two-dimensional look. It could be painted on the wall.

'What's happened to the jug?' Olive asks.

'The vase?' Jim runs two fingers down the bulge of its side. 'Nothing,' he says.

'Ahh.'

'You've got your clothes on.'

'Yes.'

'Are you ill?'

'I think I must be.'

'Well what sort of ill?' he sighs.

'Perhaps I'm going crazy like my mother.' Completely without intention these words slip out.

'Jesus, Olive. What sort of shit is this?'

'I was joking.'

'It's not remotely funny.'

'No.' Olive slides from the bed onto the floor. She sits pulling on her slippers.

'You look like a child doing that.'

'Doing what?'

He smiles. 'Putting your slippers on sitting on the floor.'

Olive looks up at him and is filled with silent gratitude. 'I think I need a rest.'

'But a rest from what?'

'I don't know. I feel so tired.'

'Seems to me you have to be tired from something. Or tired of something. You don't have that much to do these days. The kids are gone.'

'Yes, the children are gone.'

'What is it, then?'

'I don't know.'

'You keep on saying you don't know.'

'I had to kill the blackbird.' Olive catches the rising note of helplessness.

'What the hell?'

'The blackbird in the garden. I had to kill it today.'

'Why?'

'Blood.' The word settles awkwardly in the room.

'What do you mean, blood? What does blood mean?'

'It had a hole in its chest. It was bleeding. It bled all over my hand.'

'And how did you kill it?'

'I drowned it in a bucket.'

'I see.'

'The yellow plastic bucket.'

'Mm.'

'And when it was dead its head went all loose and hung right over on its breast as if its neck was broken. But I didn't touch its neck. It just drowned.'

'I see. And then you retired to bed for the day with a fit of morbid depression.'

'Morbid depression?'

His hands spread open. 'Well what is going on?'

'I don't know. I was looking through some photographs.'

'And?'

'I felt.'

'Felt what?'

'A bit sort of low,' she says.

'And then what?'

'And then I had to kill the blackbird.'

'Photos of what?'

'Mum and Father.'

'Olive, that was years ago.'

'I know. I was just thinking about them, that's all. I do think of them sometimes. There's a photograph of Mum at the hospital. She got so fat. Her eyes look like currants.'

'Well don't let it upset you. Whether she was fat or not makes no difference to you now. She's been dead for twenty-five years.'

'It's more like thirty.'

'Quite a while,' Jim says.

'Silly, isn't it?'

'It certainly is.'

'I'm sorry,' Olive says quietly. Her mind is back on the sensation she had felt upon waking.

'Not now,' were the words on her lips. It wasn't a dream so much as a feeling. A disinclination to be roused from the blankness of such heavy sleep. She'd have liked to stay there for a long time.

'What are we going to eat?' Jim says.

'Eat? It will have to be eggs, I suppose. It's too late.'

'Fine.'

'I'll make an omelet.'

In the kitchen Olive breaks eggs into a bowl. The halved shells rock on the bench. Pushing them aside with her hand she knocks a tomato. The plump fruit falls to the floor. Its sound on polished wood is ripe and soft.

'Have you seen the avocado tree?' she says, carrying the food through. 'There's something wrong with it.'

Egg quivers on the serving spoon and slides onto a plate.

'No.' He takes the plate.

'It doesn't look too good.'

'Has it got a blight?'

'What blight?'

'Any blight.'

'I don't know what it is. Will you have a look sometime?'

'Sure. Where's the salt?' Already his mouth is full.

'Ah, I forgot it. I forget things all the time these days. Yesterday I poured a cup of tea then straight away turned around and poured another one. I was sitting there with two cups of tea.'

'Which one did you drink?'

'Both of them.'

Jim laughs. The expression on his face as he eats is his customary one.

Olive looks over her shoulder through the open kitchen door. The tomato is still on the floor near the fridge. A faint line of watery juice gleams along the split in its side. The shadow is larger than the tomato.

Tonight everything looks different. Something is wrong with the light. Change back! The omelet like the strange light in the bedroom is very yellow.

'Jesus, Olive!' Jim drops his fork with a clatter. 'There's bloody birdshit on the table!'

CHAPTER TWO

AUTUMN DRAWS ON. Late one evening the twins come home. One minute the house is still as if already settled for the night and in the next it is charged with energy.

Big young women, they have inherited Jim's height and colouring. Heather's eyes are blue where Ruth's tend to green and her lips curve more but the differences are slight. They exude an equal vitality.

'How are things at the hospital?' Jim asks.

'The place is full of bloody nutters.'

'They're all crazy.'

'Except us.'

'You're working in a psychiatric ward?'

'No, we're not.'

'That's the point.' Heather throws her head back and roars. The exposed aspect of her throat is pale.

The young bloom, Olive is thinking.

Reclining each at opposite ends of the sofa they file their fingernails. Their legs and feet overlap casually. At a certain angle Heather's nail-file catches the light and flashes out as if with a light of its own.

Ruth stops to pick at a speck on her thumb-nail where the red polish is beginning to lift. From Olive's position the bare spot looks blue, but as Ruth's hand moves around she sees it is the soft pink one would expect.

It is the pink of the old camellia at the gate. Not the exuberant hue of tender buds but the pale blush of full bloom. The twins are more beautiful than ever. Their skin is smooth and lush.

But in some way now they are as strangers. Where did they come from, Olive wonders. From inside my body?

The thought is too abstract and strange. She looks at them. These big daughters.

'When I was a child,' she says, 'I went with my father to visit Mum in hospital and while we were waiting a man came into the room and urinated into somebody's slippers. He was a little Chinese man. My father didn't say a thing.'

'Pissed in a pair of slippers.' The twins laugh. 'That's mild.'

'They were brand new fleecy-lined blue plaid slippers. The urine just sat in them like in boats. It didn't soak through.'

'How deep was it?' Jim asks.

'Why do you want to know that?'

'Just wondering.'

'About half an inch, I suppose.'

'In each one?'

'Yes, both of them.'

'Half an inch of pee in a pair of brand-new fleecy-lined blue plaid slippers. Forty years ago. That's not bad for someone who can't even remember what day of the week it is!' Jim winks to indicate his words are not unkindly meant.

'Father shocked me more than the man in a way,' Olive says. 'He ignored the whole incident. "The climbing roses will be out soon, Olive." That's what he said to me at the time. I thought he should do something or tell someone but he didn't, and when we left it was still there.'

'The climbing roses will be out soon, Olive.' It comes to her now all these years later that these words are the saddest she has ever heard.

'We had a woman in the other day who wanted to have her artificial hip joint removed,' Ruth says. 'She thinks the Post Office is trying to trace her through it.'

'I don't want to hear this story,' says Olive.

'Yes you do. A sort of internal bugging device.'

'Please, I don't want to know. The poor woman.'

Ruth jabs with her nail-file. 'You'd love to hear all about it.'

'No, I wouldn't. I loathe your horror stories. I'd really

rather not know.'

'Why?'

'Because once something is inside your head you can't get it out again.'

'Because you've got a weak stomach, you mean!'

Jim laughs along with the twins.

'I'll make a cup of tea.' Olive rises to her feet. 'There's apple pie if you'd like some.'

'Yeah.' Pulling herself upright, Heather nods. 'We're starving.'

'They feed us brown stew at the hospital.'

'All the time.'

'This brown stew. It's disgusting.'

'We only come home for the food.'

'We're staying tonight and tomorrow too.'

'I'll start cooking right away,' Olive says.

She turns the light on in the kitchen. Dishwater is still in the sink from earlier in the evening. It is cold now and greasy. Pulling the plug, she watches it drain away.

The pie is in a round tin. With a sharp knife she cuts it evenly into six pieces. Near the crust the pastry crumbles, but the blade when she withdraws it is clean. The first segment is difficult to remove but the others lift out easily.

The food is quickly consumed. Olive pours second cups of tea and passes the sugar bowl. She piles plates and spoons back onto the tray.

'Well, I might go to bed soon,' she says.

Jim nods but makes no reply. His attention swings back to Heather.

'There's this supervisor,' says Heather. 'That we hate.'

At midnight Olive leaves the three of them still talking and goes to bed. 'Look at the moon,' she calls out.

It is full and red like a blood orange.

There is no response. They have not heard. She listens to the murmur of voices through the wall.

'*Coral Island* or something like that,' says Ruth.

'A blood moon in *Coral Island*,' Olive whispers, pulling the bedcovers back. The sheets are cold.

The bright moon shines on her face. What gives the colour such strength? It is beautiful but also terrible in some way. Turning her back she pulls the blankets up under her chin.

'Winter's coming on!' she cries out.

Again there is no sign they have heard. Why don't they hear me? Their voices swell into laughter again.

'The climbing roses will be out soon, Olive!' she shouts and then her hand is up over her mouth.

Shocked, she rolls over and back into the moonlight. Why say a thing like that? It makes no sense.

She squirms in the bed. Her legs are aching. Ahh. She cannot tell if it is bone pain or muscle. Such distinctions blur and merge in the night. The throbbing seems to spread right through.

A cold wind moves over the bed. Lying in the dark, she watches pale clouds race past the bloodshot moon. From black they swirl into the light, then off again.

She is watching that and her thoughts are on winter. Another winter on its way, she thinks.

Olive wakes at dawn. A dog barks in the distance. Thin light spikes through gaps in the bamboo blind.

The blind was up last night, she remembers vaguely. After a time she is sinking back into sleep. A dream begins.

Olive and her friend Dorothy are walking along a street. There are shops on either side but they are not the local shops. Pumpkins are stacked on the footpath.

All these pumpkins, Olive thinks, stepping around. They are the small, sweet variety. Some are flat and others are round but the skin textures are constant. The green sides are ridged. Withered stalks protrude from the tops.

A number of army officials appear. They all wear the same drab uniform and their faces too seem much the same. At first they are milling about then they set off purposefully. They are leading a band of emaciated women up the street.

They must be the daughters, Olive guesses, although the women are not young. She watches them approach. They weave around the piles of pumpkins and their movements are slow with fatigue. There is no energy. Their feet are bare and knotted.

Dorothy turns away and enters a building to one side. She is climbing a flight of stairs. Olive follows. She bounds up the stairs without effort as if lifted from below. They enter a room full of women. One of them is a well-known doctor. She approaches Olive without hesitation.

'You look pale,' she says.

'I'm not well,' Olive explains.

The doctor holds some sort of pink fruit or a cake. Her hair is cut in such a way that when she moves her head it swings out in a glossy arc. She bites into the fruit and cream extrudes from the other end. A ridged tube emerges. The folds in the cream are the same marks as on the pumpkin skins.

Olive looks away in disgust. The woman moves into her field of vision again. A fleck of cream sticks to the side of her nose.

'How can you eat?' asks Olive. It seems quite wrong.

Shiny hair swings out and the doctor takes another bite. Her enjoyment is evident.

'How can you eat?' she asks again, then she sees that everyone is eating. There are tables covered with food. Sandwiches are arranged on plates and cakes decorated with yellow peach slices.

'Dorothy!' she cries, but her friend has gone.

I'll just leave, she thinks, spinning around. The room leads out into a forest. She finds herself on a path between thin trees and she is alone.

A stream runs alongside and she sets off following its course. Clear water runs over banks of sand and stone. Smaller tributaries enter from the other side and the volume increases. Green plants reach out over the water. There has never been a bird in this place or any sound other than the flowing of water.

At a certain point the stream drains down into a pool. The feeling is different here. Square black rocks form a bank.

Olive moves closer as if mesmerised. The bottom isn't visible. It is too deep for that. I might go in, she thinks. It's not a serious thought but her feet are on the rocks then entering the water.

At first her legs slide in. Ripples glide out. She sees the concentric rings spread then that picture disappears as her body slips down. The surface closes overhead.

There is no decision or effort involved. It just happens.

The pool is cold and deep and she sinks slowly. The sensation of being submerged in water is pleasant. I'll just sink and sink. Drift down into the easiness. The surface is a skin above and through it the sky is a pale and distorted sheet. The colours are separate but bound together. The water is murky and green. Lazy bubbles rise.

I don't know. It is so vague and simple. Inevitably the direction is a gentle descent.

Suddenly something is tight around her arm. She recoils, reaching out, but the grip will only tighten further. She is pulled up through green black water to the surface and beyond the surface into air. The water runs off her limbs. All the weight of her body returns.

Someone has reached into the pool from the bank and caught her by the arm. She cries out in fright and she's twisting and turning but there is no relief. Black rocks slither underneath and now she's on the path.

The person stands over her. 'If you stay in the water you will die.' The words aren't audible in a physical sense but are communicated nevertheless with force.

Her fear grows to terror. The figure is shadowy. She cannot see a face. Is it a man or a woman? Some sort of garment covers their head.

Rolling over there is nothing to be seen now but the water. It spreads and spreads into an ocean. The surface glitters black.

In panic Olive wakes up. She is out of bed and rushing from the room before she realises. She stops in the dining room and her hands are pressed flat on the wall then she's heading for the bathroom. She vomits into the toilet. The quantity is meagre but her throat stings and the taste is foul in her mouth.

Straightening, she steps back until she's leaning on the wall. There is a thin layer of dust along the top of the cistern.

A dream, a dream, she thinks. Only a dream. But the

cold feeling of water is still slick on her hands. She holds them beneath the hot tap for as long as she can. Her breath steadies.

In the bedroom bars of sunlight coming through the blind are stronger now. They make yellow stripes on the bed and over the mound which is Jim's body.

Olive looks at the bedside clock then looks again. An hour has passed since she woke at dawn. It seemed the dream had begun as soon as she'd gone back to sleep. Could such a dream last for so long? There is no way of telling.

The house is still. Jim sleeps heavily. His lips are apart but he breathes through his nose. In the front his teeth are crooked. The distortion is not unattractive.

Reaching over, Olive touches them. They are dry against her finger and she withdraws.

I'll go into the garden, she resolves. Taking a jacket she moves quietly along the hall.

Outside, the top lawn is divided by the shadow of the house. One side of the garden is dark and damp with dew while the other side is sunny and warm.

It is the bright side to which she is attracted. The sky stretches overhead. It is a vast covering of clear cobalt. It will be a fine day on earth.

The chrysanthemums are still shaded by the wall while the other flowerbeds are in the sun.

Weeds have grown up amongst the cornflowers. The cornflower leaves are silver-grey and the weeds are green. Flowers are festive spots of pink and blue throughout.

Dropping the jacket Olive sets to work in her nightdress. The weeds are succulent and come up easily in her hands. Although their grip is firm the soil is soft. Immediately they are pulled their lustre fades and the scent of freshly turned soil rises from the roots. As the sun warms the earth the smell intensifies.

Resting for a moment, Olive looks around. At the bottom of the garden the lawn stretches smoothly beneath taller trees and is dappled by their shadow. Beauty is everywhere. But no. The dying tree. It bursts out to stand there before her.

How could I have forgotten? That something is rotting at the bottom of the garden. And the feeling of the morning changes back. She is sickened by the sight of the dying tree. The tree that is me. Don't think it.

But there it is, in front of her eyes. Drooping and forlorn. Strangely, the avocado doesn't appear to be without new growth. Each branch is tipped with masses of buds but at some point before the leaves ripen they blacken and collapse.

The larger leaves were yellow but now they are dull. They hang from the branches like rags. This change has brought an even more foreboding aspect.

'What are you doing? Hello there, hello!' Heather and Ruth call from the top of the garden.

Spinning on her heel Olive moves away. She walks in one random direction across the lawn then turns and retraces her steps.

'Hup two three four,' Heather cries.

'What are you doing?'

'Weeding,' she replies.

'Great day.'

Sleepily the twins bend and stretch in the sun. Below the pale cotton of their nightdresses their legs are still tanned but they move with caution. Already their feet are winter-soft. They pick their way slowly down the path.

Olive holds her breath. Don't come any closer. Keep away. Don't look at the tree.

'How about the cornflowers?' she shouts.

The twins start and look up.

'What?' Ruth says.

'The cornflowers.'

'You've been weeding already.' Heather prods at the pile of weeds. They are quite without life now and diminished in size.

'Yes, a bit.'

'Cornflowers are nice.'

'Yes. Did you sleep well?'

'Sure did.' Ruth yawns. Her teeth are perfect. 'How come you're up so early?'

'I had a dream. It woke me up.'

Now barely an hour later certain images from the dream are still clear but much of the detail has slipped away. The feeling of sinking in water remains sharp, but sharper again is the shock of nearly dying by just not thinking. A casual mistake. To so easily let a life go.

'How long do you think a dream lasts for?' she says. 'In real time.'

'Not long, I don't think,' says Ruth.

'An hour? Half an hour?'

'No, not that long.'

'Only minutes,' Heather says.

Jim comes down the path in his pyjamas. His hair is tousled. 'Good morning! Are we having breakfast out here?'

'No, we're not. I'm just coming in. I've been weeding the cornflowers.'

'We've not had pink before.'

'No, they're new.'

'The blue are better.'

'Perhaps. But the pink are pretty too.'

'If you like that sort of thing,' he says. 'Jesus, that tree is in a bit of a state.'

Olive's breath draws in. 'Leave it for now.'

But Jim continues striding down the path. He walks on the grass in his slippers. He is pushing against the avocado trunk. Leaves float down, tacking from left to right in a gentle descent.

Reaching up, he rips at a small branch. At first the break is incomplete and he wrenches it. Bark pulls off down the trunk in a long shred. Running his fingers over it Jim examines the wound.

Olive can barely watch.

'Still green on the inside.' He drops the branch to the ground.

'It never fruited anyway,' Ruth says.

'It never fruited anyway.' The words cut like a blade.

'But it's years before they fruit!' says Olive.

'How old is it?'

'We put it in when you girls were babies. That makes it twenty years.'

'It's had long enough,' says Heather. 'How come your eye's all twitching?'

'My eye's not twitching. Nothing's twitching. Look at the chrysanthemums.'

Olive sets off stumbling across the lawn. Each foot strives to trip the other up. Nobody seems to notice.

Splendid in the morning dew, the flowers are a successful diversion. Ruth picks a handful to take indoors. Her preference is for the rust-coloured blooms.

'They used to be my favourites too,' Olive says. 'But now I like the white ones best.'

'Oh no,' says Heather. 'The white ones are dead boring.'

Where the blackbird is buried the soil has already settled down. Weeds are sprouting. There is nothing to distinguish the spot from the surrounding soil.

'Look at this.' Olive holds her hand out.

'What?'

'This mark here. What do you think it is?'

'Yuk.'

'It's a liver spot,' says Ruth.

'Show the girls your bruises,' Jim demands.

'What bruises?'

'They've faded now. There's a bit of yellow on my shins, that's all. It's nothing.'

'You should have seen them,' he says. 'I've never seen bruises like it. Her legs were black and blue!'

'What happened?'

'Ah, nothing. I fell down the steps one day, that's all.'

'How?'

'I slipped. That's all. It was raining.'

'Shit. You should be more careful.'

'What causes liver spots?' asks Olive.

'A malfunctioning liver. That's what people used to think it was,' Ruth answers. 'But it's not, it's just old age.'

'Old age. I'm not that old. Do you get them on your palms?'

'Not as a rule.'

'What else could it be?'

'Oh it's a liver spot, all right.'

'I see.' With her finger Olive rubs away at the bloodstain

until the skin around it burns.

Ruth and Heather slap their knees and laugh.

'No good doing that!' Heather shouts. 'You've got it for life!'

In the afternoon Olive and Ruth sort through several boxes of fabrics. They have them on the floor in the front room.

Ruth rubs a remnant of striped material between her fingers. 'I've gone off this stuff,' she says. 'It's dated. It's useless now.'

A heavy fly drones against the window.

'A late fly,' says Olive. 'Look how slow it is.'

'What are we going to do with you?' Ruth asks.

'What do you mean?'

'Dad says you never go out, you just mope around the house the whole time.'

'I do not.' The denial is firm but Olive looks away. 'Well I suppose I do, but so what?'

'It's not good for you.'

'Why not? I was home for years with you kids.'

'But we've all left now.'

'Yes.'

'And it's time you got out and about.'

Spread on the floor the materials are bright squares. Red and yellow overlap.

'Perhaps I should make a patchwork quilt,' says Olive.

'Perhaps you should.'

'There's something about the shape of a square. But I do like circles better. If I shut my eyes and just let any image come to mind sometimes it's an egg.'

'Jesus,' says Ruth.

'I often imagine an egg these days.'

'I thought you didn't like eggs.'

'I don't like to eat them much. But it's not that. It's the shape. There's something about the shape of an egg.'

'You're not actually all that happy are you?'

Olive is jolted by the accusation. Her eyes blink. 'I am,' she says.

'Dad doesn't seem to think so.'

'Ah, I see. Did he ask you to speak to me?'

'No, of course not.'

Olive carefully folds a piece of gingham. Her fingers turn it one way, then the other. Smaller and smaller the neat square of it becomes.

Squares inside a square, she feels like muttering.

'Have you ever thought of doing voluntary work? Meals on wheels or something like that?' Ruth's gaze is unrelenting.

'I couldn't stand it.'

'Yes, you could.'

'No I couldn't.'

'You'd meet new people and get out and about a bit. It would do you good.'

'No you're wrong,' says Olive. 'I've been looking after people since I was eight years old. It's my turn now.'

'But what does that mean? You're not exactly doing anything.'

'I'm busy all day.'

'Yeah. You muck about in the garden all day but there's got to be something else.'

For a moment the ugliness of the dying tree comes before Olive. Rotting leaves sway in the wind.

Ruth stands at the window. A curved fragment of paua hangs from one ear. Although she doesn't move the shell stirs and changes from green to blue and back to green again.

Jumping quickly to her feet, Olive spins on one heel. She leaves the room.

Her spirits are low and during dinner she makes little effort to speak. Peas fall from her fork and scatter on the table.

'What's up with you?' Jim asks.

'Nothing's up.'

He pours gravy over his food. A brown line divides the mound of mashed potato into two.

'You're being very quiet.'

'I'm tired.'

'You're tired? You'd better have an early night.'

'Yes, I will.'

Olive clears the table. She washes the dishes and leaving them to dry retires immediately to bed. She lies close to the edge of the mattress. It's not yet seven o'clock and barely dark.

In the garden the last birds still chirp. Sparrows settle in the bamboo for the night.

The twins drive off. Olive and Jim stand on the veranda and wave until their car disappears around the corner at the bottom of the street. Olive keeps her eyes on the road. There is nothing there now.

She steps back into the house. The hallway is empty. Her footsteps echo on polished wood. Is it actually darker? The lounge has the same feeling.

She wanders around switching on the lights.

'What are you doing?' Jim follows her from room to room. 'We don't need lights on in the middle of the day.'

'It seems dark. The house feels brown.'

'Brown?' He glances over his shoulder.

'I don't mean it looks brown. It feels brown.'

'It's no darker than usual.' He goes about switching the lights off.

'I'm going to do some baking,' Olive calls. 'I think I'll make a cake.'

A warm cake to fill the house with sweet cooking smells. A nourishing cake to drive the brown away.

She takes the large bowl and arranges ingredients on the kitchen bench. Cutting butter and sugar together she softens them in hot water and beats the mixture with a wooden spoon until it is pale. She breaks three eggs into the bowl. The yolks remain intact and she prods them so they break and leak out across the batter in slow yellow rivers. Flour and the other ingredients blend in.

The cake is in the oven now and the rich smell of baking leaches slowly out to fill the kitchen.

Tentatively Olive explores the rest of the house. The atmosphere has changed fractionally. It feels more like beige now. Not a pleasant pink beige but something yellower.

Baking always works, she thinks, opening a door. It makes the feeling better. But today its success is only partial.

In the hall mirror she catches her own eye. It is too late to pull away. What's going on? Sad dark eyes stare back. Something is changing. It's the light. The light is wrong.

The eyes flicker but the expression is the same. Looking out and through. Her mind is choked with questions. Cloudy questions. I don't even know what they are. And the eyes just stare. Lost. It is the only word.

'Jim, Jim!' she calls.

There is no reply.

'Jim, where are you?'

The house is empty.

'Jim!'

The cake sticks to the tin and comes out torn along the bottom. It is low and heavy and a jagged crack runs along the top. The edges of the crack are a shade deeper than the rest.

Jim comes into the kitchen. 'Chocolate, is it?'

'Where were you?'

'When?'

'Just before.'

'Outside. Is it chocolate?'

'No, it's coconut.'

He prods it with his finger. 'It looks pretty bad.'

'Shall we go for a walk?'

He looks up. 'Now?'

'We could go down to the beach.'

'I suppose so,' Jim says. 'Give me ten minutes.'

The tide is unusually full. Water laps up almost as far as the sea wall. The harbour bridge rises large and grey. It dominates the view. Traffic is a steady hum.

Cans and plastic bags litter the narrow strip of sand and the water supports a frothy line of mustard-coloured scum. A small boy runs through and into the cleaner area beyond. There are no waves. The child's palms slap down on the surface.

Usually a pleasant scene, today it is cheerless. The light over the harbour is oppressive. It is the harsh light of a Sunday afternoon.

Overhead a gull circles and calls its lonely cry.

'Sea air,' Jim says. He takes an extravagant breath. 'Marvellous.'

Looking at the same thing Olive is uncomfortably aware that she and Jim see something quite different. The thought makes her nervous.

Nearby a Maori girl of fourteen or fifteen years sits staring out over the water. She smokes a cigarette. Between each inhalation she taps the ash off with her finger and when the cigarette is almost finished Olive watches her take another one from a packet and light it from the butt. Her knuckles are blue with tattoos.

Jim follows her gaze. 'That's dreadful,' he says nodding at the girl.

'What is?'

'I read in the paper this morning that less men in New Zealand are smoking but the number of women who smoke has increased.'

'I'm not surprised.'

'It goes to show that women are weaker than men.'

'Weaker?'

'Weaker willed. Women have less willpower than men. It's what the statistics indicate.'

'Perhaps women are less happy than men,' Olive says, glancing across at the girl drawing deeply on her cigarette.

'Less happy. Do you think so? If women are less happy than men then whose fault might it be?'

Turning away, Olive scrapes up a handful of pebbles. She throws them one at a time into the sea and they hit with a dull sound as if the sea isn't water at all but something of an oilier nature.

'I'm glad our four are too sensible to smoke,' Jim says.

'Presuming it's a matter of sense.'

'What else do you put it down to then?'

'Annette eats, you know,' Olive blurts out.

'What do you mean, Annette eats? We all eat, don't we?'

'She eats too much.'

'She's greedy, then.'

'No, she's not greedy. She's full of hungry ghosts and

it's not her fault.'

'Hungry ghosts. Jesus, Olive! What crap is this now?'

'She has some sort of compulsive eating problem.'

'How do you know?'

'A mother notices these things.'

'That's why she's fat then?'

'Yes.'

'It's two years she's been in Australia now,' says Jim.

'I know.'

'Well, she might not be fat anymore.'

'She is.'

'But isn't she always dieting, or something?'

'Yes.'

'I'm afraid I don't understand.' Distaste distorts his face.

'Look at that.' Olive lifts her foot. 'My shoe's split along the sole.'

'They look dreadful.'

She pushes one finger into the split. The rubber has perished. 'I'll get some new ones this week. I saw some black boots.'

'Don't get black.'

'They'd be good for winter.'

'Not black,' Jim says. 'Get camel, it's a much nicer colour.'

They sit in silence. Two seagulls glide down and land on the beach. They pick their way through the rubbish. One rushes at the other, its neck aggressively outstretched.

Jim nudges Olive with his elbow. 'Look,' he hisses. 'Two cigarettes at once.'

Two cigarettes together. Olive's shoulders sink. 'So what?' she says. 'It's nothing to do with us.'

'But it *is* rather strange.'

'No, it's not.'

Jim snorts. 'It bloody well is.'

'I don't know.'

'You know it is.'

'All right, all right.'

While one cigarette is in the girl's mouth another is in her hand. She puffs first on one and then on the other.

Olive is overcome with compassion for the girl but she wants to move away.

'Let's walk along the beach.' Jumping up too quickly she bends forward. She is brushing down her skirt as if that was her intention in the first place.

Slowly they wander along at the water's edge and soon reach the end of the sand. Dull slabs of sandstone pile up into a bluff at the end of the bay.

'There's something wrong with that girl,' says Olive.

'She's too young to smoke. That's all that's wrong with her.'

'But she seems disturbed or something.'

'Mm.' Jim drags a stick through a puddle of weak mud.

Olive looks desperately up and down the beach.

Jim begins to whistle.

Back at the sea wall the foreshore is deserted. The girl has vanished as silently as she came.

A mass of cigarette butts litter the ground. Some of them are barely burned and broken in the middle and others have been smoked right down to the filter. One of them is still alight. A watery mark encircles the end.

Olive thinks of the girl's full lips. It seems they were pale like a child's, or blue with cold.

A thin column of smoke winds gently upwards from the cigarette and disappears into the still grey afternoon air.

CHAPTER THREE

OLIVE POURS MILK into a mug of coffee and whirls it with the handle of a spoon. The liquids blend and she continues stirring. The spoon grates on the rough insides of the mug.

Withdrawing it, she presses the burning handle to her neck. The pain is intense for a moment, then as quickly the metal cools. She stares out the window.

'You never go out. You mope around the house the whole time.' Ruth's words of the previous week come back.

I'll go to town then, she thinks suddenly.

Half an hour later she is setting off for the bus stop. The front door bangs behind and her heels click over the veranda and down the front stairs. Her shoes are stylish but uncomfortable. The pointed toes restrict her feet and the heels are too high.

Part way up the hill she stops. A red hibiscus grows on the verge nearby. The bush is untrimmed and has formed an awkward shape but the flowers are as large as saucers. Deep crimson in the throat, they lighten to vermilion along the petal. The gradation in colour gives an impression of immense softness.

It is the only hibiscus in the street still in flower. The others are long finished. The old lady carries on.

The strength in the bush is unmatched by anything Olive feels. She stands looking out over the harbour. On the other side the land is bleached. The bush-covered hills are dull and house roofs glint all around. Colours are robbed of their richness. The light is bad again.

Spinning about, she retraces her steps to the house. Go to town, she thinks. Stay home. It would be easier inside where the light is muted. I will find a quiet corner.

Ahh. She sighs and walks back up the hill. Her left leg feels numb. It drags, or is it the shoes?

As she passes the hibiscus this time the scarlet flowers have lost their gentle aspect. They are red as blood and open and savage.

In town the footpaths are crowded with people and shop windows are bright with displays. Olive wanders along and watches faces flood by. The abundance is confusing.

'Lost,' she whispers. It is the only word. All these people. They seem to know exactly where they're going. I don't feel like one of them.

A picture in the window of a print shop catches her eye, then a new surge of people pass between. She is waiting and pushing through until her hand is on the glass.

The picture is of an old oak tree naked for the winter. Each branch and twig reaches into the air. Soft in its form, the tree contrasts sharply with the barren landscape of the background. It is a living thing in a hostile environment.

Olive enters the shop. Two men wait to be served at the counter. Amongst the prints displayed on the walls is another one by the same printmaker. The resemblance in style is strong.

In this one a sea lies calm below a sky turbulent with gathering storm. The scene is simple but dynamic.

Olive's eye is drawn to the horizon. Smoky green sea meets a line of blue-grey sky. At one point the darker colour of sky has leached into a fine haze and run into the sea, giving an impression of rain. Whether the effect is intentional or accidental there is no way of knowing. It is moody and somehow beautiful.

'Calm before the storm', the print is called. The name on the card is that of a man.

Ah, a man. Olive looks back to the print with surprise. Although she is without a picture of the artist there is an undeniably female element in the scene. Both the pent energy of the storm and the tranquillity of the ocean have a female strength.

She admires it for a long time before leaving the shop. Back in the street she sets off walking down the footpath.

Where shall I go now?

A group of people are gathered at a chemist shop entrance. They stand looking down at a man. He lies on his back, halfway in and halfway out of the door.

Olive pauses. Her eyes are on him also. He is well dressed but his socks are odd. The fall has twisted and pulled his trouser legs up from the bottom. One sock is brown and the other is green. He is frozen and the other people around him are also inert.

Should I walk on, Olive thinks, glancing up. Offer assistance. Why does nobody move? Then she realises. The man is dead. A man walking down the street on his way somewhere has dropped dead in a shop doorway.

Olive moves quickly on. Red as blood and open and savage. But no aspect of this death is like that. It is neither bright like blood nor torn and open but colourless. A dreary city death.

A man who got up today like any other day and kissed his wife and walked out the door. And now he's dead.

'He probably had weetbix for breakfast,' Olive mutters absurdly.

And his wife won't know yet. She can see her at home sitting at the table with a cup of tea and a cracker with cheese. She will be planning the evening meal and writing out her shopping list. In five minutes the phone will ring and her safe world will shatter.

Olive is aware of how much the woman in her imaginings looks like herself.

Now nearly at the bottom of Queen Street she is unable to recall with clarity any detail of the dead man other than the fact that his socks were odd. He has retreated, but the odd socks remain. One of brown and one green.

She is bothered by it. As if he wasn't loved, she thinks. I must have been wrong about the wife.

Reaching the end of the street Olive crosses at the lights and makes her way up the other side. She is tired and looks around for somewhere to stop for coffee. A neon sign winks and she enters the building. Selecting sandwiches in a hurry she waits while the proprietor pours her coffee.

A narrow flight of stairs leads to a small second floor. The salt and pepper shakers are white cylinders and the tablecloths are pink. A single carnation has been placed in a vase at the centre of each table. They are the pastel shades. The effect is plain but inviting. She is relieved to sit down.

Wriggling her feet free from the shoes she looks around. There is nobody else in the room. The rush for lunch is over and the rush for afternoon tea yet to begin.

As she bites into a tomato sandwich her thoughts return to the dead man. One sock of brown and one of green. And a portion of leg where it showed between one sock and his trouser leg was meagre and winter-white. Thinking of it now, it seems the flesh was hairless.

The sandwiches are damp and spongy and Olive pushes the plate away. The coffee is hot and strong.

A young woman enters the room and chooses a table to the rear.

Olive becomes aware of a scent. It fills her with a curious pleasure. Pennyroyal, she thinks. Here in the city? Where is it coming from? She half turns in her chair.

The young woman has no look of the country about her. She takes her glasses off and polishes them then puts them back on and sips a tall glass of orange juice. She spreads papers out on the table in front of her and marks them with a red pen.

Ah, Olive thinks, breathing in deeply. The scent has not dispersed. It touches at something good. So sweet. It triggers a feeling buried a long time ago.

Pennyroyal growing on the farm. Springing up amongst grass in the paddocks and taller and lush in dappled shade on the banks of the creek. Fragrant plants crushing beneath bare summer feet and bees busy in the lavender flowers.

Long sunny days and Mother baking apple cake. She was happy then.

Ahh. Breathing in the smell she experiences a powerful conviction that all is well in the world. That feelings can change so much. The weight of the man's death disappears as if by magic. Olive is enormously comforted.

I'll buy the print! The thought leaps into her mind and

she is scarcely able to contain her excitement. Leaping to her feet she hurries down the stairs and through the door back onto the street. She walks briskly, keeping pace with the people on the footpath.

Passing the chemist shop she stops and looks down at the black rubber mat where the man had lain. Fine ridges run from one side to the other. There is a thin round of orange peel on the centre. The inside is grey and it curls at the edges.

Was it there when the man fell to the ground? If it was, his body would have covered it.

An abundantly fat man steps from the shop and stands on the mat. He bends forward and looks down the street then turns and peers in the other direction. The orange peel is scuffed away to one side. He waddles off.

Business is as usual. There is nothing to tell that a man died here today.

Olive steps into the print gallery. The picture is still on the wall. It is even more dynamic than her memory of it. Both the sky and ocean are vigorous with energy.

A man leans against a desk.

'I'll take that one,' Olive says.

'A quick decision.'

'Ah . . . I came in and looked at it before.'

'Did you?' The man takes it from the wall and wraps it in a large sheet of brown paper. He secures the corners with sellotape.

'Thank you.'

'It's expensive,' the man says. 'But his work's in great demand these days. It's rather macabre.'

'Macabre?' Does he mean the picture?

'It often happens like that.'

'What does?'

'People take more interest when you die. It's jolly good for sales.'

'Dead. Who's dead?'

'Oh, the artist,' he says. 'I presumed you knew about the artist.'

'No, I'm afraid I don't. I just saw the print and liked it.'

'Oh I see.' He hands the parcel over. 'He died recently.'

'Was he an old man?'

'He was only in his early thirties. He took his own life. Suicide by hanging. There was a bit about it in the papers at the time.' The man lowers his voice. His manner is conspiratorial. 'Apparently he lived a complicated life,' he says.

Olive clutches the parcel against her body tenderly as if it were a child.

'Christ,' Jim says. 'What did it cost?'

'Don't you like it?'

'No, I can't say I do.'

'I like it very much.'

'It's exaggerated,' he says. 'And it's a tedious scene. But if you like it, that's fine.'

'How can you think it's tedious?'

'Easily. Have you ever seen a sky like that?'

'All the time,' Olive cries.

Jim looks across at her. 'Where are you going to hang it?'

'I don't know. The man at the gallery said that the artist lived a complicated life.'

'Did he?'

'What do you imagine he would have meant by that?'

'He could have meant anything.'

'Yes. He's dead.'

'The artist is dead?'

'Yes.'

Jim turns back to his newspaper.

High above the flat green sea of the picture, inky storm clouds twist and roll with a violence of their own.

In the morning Olive takes the print up the narrow stairs to the attic room. Keep it away from Jim. Hide it away. His dislike is a taint.

This is the right place for it to be. The room is quite bare. The walls and sloping ceiling are painted white and the floor is unpolished wood. Two small windows open outwards and the view from them is also plain. It is a pattern of roofs varied by the tops of large trees bursting up against stark angles of corrugated iron and chimneys. Most of the rooftops are the same dull red but some are grey and one is lilac. The shapes they make are geometrical. Parts of the harbour show in between.

The window sill is scarred by pencil marks made by Jim as a child. The lead has faded but the indentations are clear. Olive touches the marks fondly. They have the look of sea birds on a long, flat coast. Pied stilts picking in a low tide. Their legs are thin and jointed like sticks.

It seems curious to think of the attic room as part of the same house. It is separate in every sense.

Olive steps back to view the picture on the wall. The emptiness of the room breathes an even greater vitality into the storm.

Ahh, she thinks. It looks so good. I can almost hear it. The quiet rumble of a gathering fury.

Sitting on the floor she turns her gaze to the window. From here the rooftops are lost. All that can be seen is the sky. It is the usual blue of a fine April day. White clouds ripple across.

But something else is happening. Another layer of cloud, lower and finer, moves with speed in an opposing direction. A drama of energy and movement unfolds. Olive watches as it constantly changes. There is nothing else she is aware of.

Finally invisible currents sweep the sky clean. No cloudy traces remain. The sky is clear blue as before.

Ahh, so tired. Rolling over, Olive stretches on the floor. Her eyes shut. Beneath her back the boards are hard but the room is warm and she soon drifts from drowsiness to sleep.

When she awakens the sky is overcast again. Beneath the window the marks on the sill stand out darkly. Sea birds pick on the long flat coast.

She runs her tongue on the back of her teeth. Jim is coming home. The thought leaps up and spins her around. In the middle of the day? He can't be. But he is. There seems no doubt.

Downstairs a door slams. Panic tightens her throat. He is home.

Looking to the sky intently this time, Olive can see that the change which occurred while she slept has not come about by a thickening of cloud but is due rather to the natural fading of early evening.

'Midday,' she mutters. 'I thought it was midday.'

A terrible distortion of time has occurred. How long did I watch the sky? And how many hours asleep on the floor?

Olive is appalled by what must be the answers to these questions.

'I'm sorry,' she tells Jim. 'But dinner will be late.'

'Have you been busy?'

'Yes.'

'What have you been doing?'

'This and that.'

'That tells me a lot.'

'Ah . . . I went to town.'

'Two days in a row. You're getting to be quite a gay thing.'

Olive takes a meat pie from the freezer and puts it straight into the oven. Unwashed dishes from the morning still clutter the bench.

During the meal Jim brings the subject up again. 'I'm glad to see you're getting out of the house,' he says. 'It's about time.'

'Yes, I know. Actually I've had an idea. I thought I might decorate the attic room for myself.'

'Are you going to start sleeping up there?'

'No, of course not. But I thought it would be quite nice to have a special room of my own.'

'What for? The house is full of rooms.'

'I know.'

'Direct your interests out of the house.'

'I'll do that too. It was just an idea I had.'

'Well it makes no odds to me. What are you going to do up there?'

'I was thinking of a sort of studio.'

'Do you mean to paint or something?'

'I might.'

For a moment the muscles tense around Jim's eyes but

his question remains unvoiced. His attention returns to the food. 'This pie is disgusting,' he says.

'What's wrong?'

'It's lukewarm in the middle.'

'Are you sure?'

'Of course I'm sure. It's tepid.'

'Mine seems all right.'

'I can't eat it,' he says. 'But the potato is passable.'

'I'm sorry.'

A vase of cornflowers sits at the centre of the table. Knowing Jim's preference Olive had chosen only the blue.

From her seat she can see out into the garden. Both the pink and blue bloom prolifically. They are lighter spots in the dark.

Although Olive can't see her face the girl at the counter of the corner dairy is familiar.

'A packet of Benson and Hedges,' the girl says. Her voice is a mere whisper.

Taking the cigarettes she makes payment with a handful of loose change. By his abrupt manner the shopkeeper makes his displeasure apparent.

It is the girl from the beach. The girl with the cigarettes. She steps past. Her shoulders are so narrow. She is small enough to be taken up in Olive's arms.

Counting the money the shopkeeper bangs coins one by one into the till. The girl stands to the rear.

He speaks without looking up. 'What can I do for you, Olive?'

From behind comes the crinkling sound of cellophane.

'A packet of Benson and Hedges,' Olive blurts out.

She stands there rigid. What am I saying? It is a message for the girl. It's all right. You'll be all right.

But there is no sound now and Olive is turning. The shop is empty. The girl has slipped out.

'You don't smoke, do you?' the shopkeeper says.

'What's that?'

'You don't smoke.'

'They're not for me.'

'I didn't think you did.'

'Ah no.'

'And how are the twins?' he asks, running a hand across the top of his head. His hair is black but his moustache is red.

'They're very well. Thank you.'

'You're lucky,' he says. 'Yes, you're lucky indeed.'

By the time Olive steps outside the girl has disappeared. Clutching the cigarettes she is alone on the footpath. Bread, she thinks. I meant to buy a loaf of bread. She turns as if to re-enter the shop but then changes her mind.

In the quiet of the attic room Olive examines the box of cigarettes. The shape is neat and compact and fits well in her hand. Inside, twenty filtertips make a pleasing arrangement.

Sliding one out she places it between her lips and strikes a match. The smoke is acrid but something of the ritual is agreeable.

As Olive exhales, the smoke drifts upwards and is sucked out through the open window. In the clear air outside it dissolves.

The cigarette makes her feel quite ill. It is only partly burnt down. She stubs it out. Shutting her eyes she stretches out on the floor. Nausea creeps in her stomach and her head reels.

The image of the egg is there before her spinning around and around. It stands out alone in the dark. The shape is perfect. Darker flecks speckle the shell.

Go away, go away.

It won't go away.

The sound of it spinning in space is the sound of no noise at all.

Olive drifts into sleep and into a dream. The first sensation is one of rolling. She is on the deck of a boat. It moves slowly through deep green water towards an island on the horizon.

Olive tries to keep her eyes on this place. All hope rests there. Enormous waves break against the lump of land sending sheets of spray high into the air. Troubled seas batter the shore.

A small girl appears alongside. Whether or not she is one of her own children Olive is unsure. It makes little difference. It doesn't occur to her to examine the child.

At first they are in an area of partial shelter but at a certain point the vessel passes from the calm into a mountainous swell. A cold wind rips. The sensation of foreboding is intense.

'Hold my hair,' Olive cries to the child. 'Hold my hair.'

And the boat rises up up. Painfully up the towering wall of water until it cannot possibly rise any more, but still the ascent continues. The deck will soon be vertical or thrown right over.

Small fingers weave through Olive's hair and the weight of the child is clay on her back. She clings on but makes no other move.

There is a sickening pause at the crest of the massive wave. A pause that will last for all time but already the sliding begins. The boat slips down down into a green-black valley of water and the angle and the speed are wrong.

That the boat will smash to pieces upon impact is a certainty.

In terror, Olive's eyes open at the very moment prior to impact. Relief sweeps across. Awakened by the violence of a terrible storm, she thinks. A tempest at sea. A dream.

Her body is braced as if to receive a blow and her palms are clammy with the dank sweat of fear.

Stiffly she stretches, rolling over on the floor. She rises up onto her elbow. Hold my hair, hold my hair. Did I call it out aloud? There is no one to have heard if I did.

A dream of a storm. What does it mean?

She turns to the picture on the wall. Her attraction to it is strong. Does it reflect some brooding rage of my own? It is an unpleasant thought and one she quickly pushes away.

In contrast to the dream the fury of the storm in the print is mild and contained.

Rising to her feet, Olive hurries from the room. Downstairs she washes her face and brushes her teeth. The aftertaste of the cigarette is dirty at the back of her mouth.

CHAPTER FOUR

OLIVE'S FRIEND DOROTHY is home from hospital but still confined to bed.

'Appendicitis,' she says. Her plump face winces. 'Do you know what the doctor said? He said it was stuffed full of watermelon seeds.'

'What was?'

'My appendix.'

'Oh.'

'"But doctor," I said. "I haven't eaten watermelon for two years."'

'Is that so?' Repelled by the image of a mass of seeds Olive looks to the floor. The carpet is tight-looped wool.

'When we were on holiday in Taupo that time. That was the last time I ate it. I think it was. I'm sure it was and that's two years ago this summer gone.'

'Is that what caused the problem?'

Dorothy heaves her body in the bed. 'It probably would have rotted anyway,' she says.

Olive looks around the room. The curtains are drawn across and the colours are anaemic. The place smells of dust. Dorothy sits propped up against a stack of pillows and her face matches the covers. Only her eyes are dark. Her body spreads in the bed.

'Would you like me to pull the curtains?' Olive asks.

'No, I don't like the light. It hurts my eyes.'

'Yes, I know what you mean. My eyes have been playing up lately. I think it's the light. It seems brighter than usual for this time of the year. It's different. They keep flicking and shutting.'

'Your eyes do?'

'Yes.'
'Shutting altogether?'
'Sort of. Sometimes. I suppose it's a sort of nervous tic.'
'What don't you want to see?'
'What's happening in my life.' The answer is spontaneous.
'Olive, that frown!'
'Oh.'
'What's the matter?'
'Ahh.'
'You look so worried.'
'It's just what you said. It rings true.'
'What does?'
'I don't want to see. It's a terrible thought.'
'No, no, Olive. I was joking.'
'Look, my eyes are twitching now. I can feel it.'
'But I wasn't being serious.'
'I know. Oh dear. But we were talking about you.'
'I'm all right really. The doctor's on at me to lose weight. He said I'll die if I don't lose weight.'
'You'll be able to.'
'Not at the rate I'm going.' Dorothy's lips spread into a smile but her eyes stay sad. 'Would you make a cup of tea?' she says.
Olive goes into the kitchen. While the jug boils she looks through the cupboards for tea-leaves. She carries the teapot and cups into the bedroom on a tray.
The flowers she had brought are on a small table beside the bed. They are the finest of the white chrysanthemums. Olive thinks of the yellow blooms and the thought is a sunny blaze. She regrets the choice of white.
'I've been dying for a cup of tea,' Dorothy says. From beneath the bedcovers she takes a brown paper bag and packets of biscuits and chocolates spill out.
They sit together sipping tea and eating chocolate biscuits.
'How's Jim?' Dorothy asks.
'I don't see him much these days.'
'Oh. Why?'

'Ah. I don't know why I said that. I see as much of him as usual. When you asked just then it seemed less. But it's not.'

'Frank picked me up from hospital on Tuesday and got me settled in bed and he was gone half an hour later. He left a paper bag on the table with a sponge cake and potato chips in it. And a little round of cheese.' Dorothy rubs at her eyes. 'He comes in late and leaves early and that's about it.'

Olive moves from her chair so she is sitting on the bed. She takes Dorothy's hand and they sit without speaking. Two middle-aged women. A clock ticks slowly on the sill.

'Silly me,' Dorothy sniffs. 'Carol rang up this morning and announced that I'm to be a grandmother. In six months time. "How do you know if it dies inside you and when do you feed them vegetables," she said. Just like that. I told her to slow down and she burst into tears. Then she said, "This is a toll call," and hung up. And here I am now sitting with you bawling away. All this crying. It's stupid.'

'It's not stupid. You're overdue for a good cry.'

'I suppose that's true.'

'So you'll be a grandmother?'

'It looks like it. It will be nice of course I think but I'd rather Carol was married or something.'

'Is she with the man?'

'I don't know. I don't think so but I didn't like to ask. She gets upset and says I'm nosey. Sometimes I think she hates me.'

'Nonsense,' Olive says. 'Of course she doesn't.'

'Frank does.'

'No, I'm sure he doesn't either.'

'Well I hate him. I know that's an awful thing to say but it's true. I've been miserable for years.'

'I know,' Olive says softly.

'Why on earth I've stood for it all these years. I don't know. What can you do? I should have left but it's too late now. It's my own fault. You're so lucky with Jim.'

'He doesn't know me.'

'What do you mean?'

'He doesn't know me. It's just something I think sometimes.'

'I still think you're lucky.'

'I don't know. Do you and Frank still sleep together?'

'Do we sleep together?'

'Do you make love, I mean?'

Dorothy looks away. Her fingers work on the bedspread, pulling loose threads and tucking them down. 'No,' she says.

'Do you mind me asking?'

'No, I don't mind. Do you?'

'Hardly ever.'

'But sometimes?'

'Yes, but do you know when we do I feel further away. How can that be? When we are close I feel further away. I feel like I'm on the other side of the world.'

Dorothy shrugs. 'When Frank dropped me off from the hospital,' she says, 'he left me this sponge cake. It was the most revolting cake I've ever seen. You've got no idea.'

'Mock cream?' Olive laughs with relief.

'Gallons of it. Mock cream and pink jam. I think he got it from the petrol station. Would you eat food from a petrol station? It tasted like kerosene. I couldn't believe it, it was so bad. As soon as he walked out the door I ate it. I ate the whole bloody thing.'

Dorothy laughs and then she cries. Tears trace the sides of her nose and run along creases to the corners of her mouth. From her chin they drop into gathered lace at her throat.

'It will be all right,' Olive says.

'Carol's only seventeen-and-a-bit and pregnant. And look at her brother. Neither of them want to know me. I must have done something terribly wrong.'

'It'll all work out fine in the end. Really it will.' The lack of conviction in Olive's words is to her own ear only too apparent.

But Dorothy dries her face on a sheet and smiles. For a moment Olive holds her. Her body is passive and soft.

'Enough of my moaning, anyway.' Propped against the pillows her lumpy body sags into an attitude of despair.

She looks so sad, yet Olive's usual feelings of affection are less today. Her hair is limp and flat. She mirrors Olive's own inner despair.

I've got to do something. I must do something. Every time Olive looks at her friend the words start up in her head.

Standing, she moves to the chrysanthemums. The container is clear cut glass. She touches their stiff petals. The centres are packed tight. The strange scent rises.

'I should have brought the yellow ones,' she says. 'They might have cheered you up a bit.'

'Oh no, I love them.'

'They're not too sombre?'

'Not at all. They're perfect. Did you grow them?'

'Yes. They grow along the garden wall.'

In this suffocating room the white flowers take on a funereal air. Against her will Olive is reminded of the dead blackbird. The feeling of it comes back. Feathers flutter in her hand. Blood is still a dark blotch on her palm.

'Perhaps all mothers have blood on their hands,' she mutters darkly.

'What was that you said?'

'Nothing. Shall we have another cup of tea?'

Dorothy ploughs through the packet of biscuits. No sooner has she swallowed than she is pressing the next one to her mouth.

Olive isn't hungry but she eats as a sign of support. I'm with you, her hand says as it reaches for another biscuit and another.

Dorothy drops the empty packet on the floor and rips another one open. These biscuits have toffee in the middle and break apart in stringy threads.

I could reduce them with my hands, Olive thinks. That would be good. To mash them up and scatter the crumbs. She takes another bite.

'They're so sweet,' says Dorothy. 'Chocolate. They make you feel like eating something salty.' Producing a bag of potato chips she rips along the top so they spill out on the bed.

After eating them they start on the round of cheese.
'Help,' Dorothy says. 'It's only a few mouthfuls each. We might as well finish it off.'
'Once you open this stuff it doesn't keep,' Olive replies.

In the evening Olive's stomach is upset and she retires to bed long before Jim. She tosses between the sheets but sleep refuses to come. She is still awake when Jim joins her.
They lie side by side in the dark. At no point do their bodies touch but Olive feels his heat. She watches the pale blotch above which is the light fitting.
'I saw Dorothy today,' she says.
'Did you?'
'Carol's having a baby.'
'When?'
'I don't know exactly. The beginning of next year, I think.'
'She's not old enough.'
'She's seventeen.'
'Jesus. Silly girl.'
'She's not silly.'
'How's Dorothy?'
'Recovering. But I don't think she's that well.'
'I see.'
'She said that when they removed her appendix it was full of watermelon seeds.'
'What do you mean?'
'I don't know. That's what she said.'
'It doesn't sound right.'
'I know. It's odd. But it was horrible. When she said it it made me think of a squirming mass of maggots.'
Jim snorts with laughter but whether in amusement or disgust Olive is unsure.
'You're the most primitive person I've ever come across,' he says.
'Primitive. Is that what you'd call it?'
'Certainly is.'
'I bought some paints on the way home from Dorothy's. Gouache and watercolours.'

'Good.'

'I thought I might try a bit of painting tomorrow. I've got to do something.'

'What are you going to paint?'

'I don't know. Perhaps I'll do you a primitive painting, shall I?'

'Not too primitive.'

His hand presses down harshly between Olive's legs.

Jim leaves for work and Olive drags a small table and chair upstairs to the attic. Placed in a corner near the window the plain furniture is unobtrusive.

She looks around and is pleased by the starkness of the room. She arranges the brushes and boxes of paints.

Sitting on the table, she lights another cigarette and draws the smoke into her lungs. As the tobacco burns down she flicks ash out through the open window. Images rise in her mind but she dismisses them one by one. I couldn't show Jim.

There is the dead blackbird. I could give it back life. It could soar in flight high in a swirling green sky. The eye will be bright again and the wing sharp. The picture is radiant in her mind. She longs to give life back to the bird.

But it would have to be kept from Jim. He wouldn't see the beauty.

She is so tired. At nine o'clock in the morning Olive is tired. Again the effect of the cigarette is extreme. She is intoxicated by it but also nauseous. Her head spins and she has to lie down.

For a short while she dozes. But I must do something. Even in a half-sleep this thought nags. It brings an increasing sense of urgency. Reluctantly, she drags herself up.

Outside in the garden Olive searches for something to paint. Beauty is all around in the cornflower bed and tender weeds and the network of branches in the orchard, but she cannot ignore the spectacle of the diseased tree.

There it stands. Pale boughs show against a darker backdrop. Black leaves flap to and fro. And the poison spreads. Now even the most peaceful corners of the garden are corrupt.

Olive takes the side path to the front garden. The border in front of the house is spared contamination. Along the boundary silver birches lose their leaves for winter. The camellia is rigid at the gate. There is no breeze to move through. Some aspect of the light has changed. It is no longer summer green and dappled but white and overexposed. There is nothing to catch the eye.

Up the street the red hibiscus is still in bloom. Each flower is a red spot on dark green. Olive sets off in that direction. Picking off a branch she takes it back down the hill and into the house.

In the attic room the colours seem even more intense. Taking a sheet of white paper she begins drawing the flowers. The pencil is new and sharp and the lines are clean.

The blooms are magnificent. Never before has she seen such fine examples. From the centre of each flower a single stamen rises, dividing finally into five minute velvet tips. The sides are powdered with yellow pollen.

Olive is moved almost to tears by their strength and beauty.

A good year for hibiscus, she thinks. But again she remembers that this bush flowers on its own. A solitary specimen. Did it begin late or is its season twice as long? Either way the stamina of the plant is evident in these blooms.

Completing the drawing Olive is surprised by the quality of her work. She steps back. It's as if the flowers have drawn themselves.

She mixes the paints, matching the colours against the blooms. The darker base lightens along the length of the petal. The first strokes are small and tight. They loosen as she goes. Changing brushes, she prepares a variety of greens for the foliage.

Hunger creeps in her stomach but it's early evening before she puts her brush down and steps back to see what is there. She is astounded. The likeness is photographic.

Walking around the room she looks at it from different angles. Without doubt the painting is very good and yet in some way she is disappointed. It has failed to fill her belly. She leaves the room.

Cutting bread in the kitchen her hand shakes violently and sends the knife clattering to the floor. She is weak with hunger.

The bread is dry but she is barely aware of that. With margarine and peanut butter it is a feast.

Jim rings from the office. 'We're having a meeting,' he says.

'Yes.'

'I'll grab something to eat in town. Do you mind? Hello, are you there?'

'Yes I'm here. That's fine.'

'You okay there?'

'Ahh, I'm fine.'

'You don't sound it.'

'I think I had some bread in my mouth.'

'You think you did?'

'No, I did.'

'I see.'

'I've done a painting.'

'Good, good,' he says. 'What is it?'

'A hibiscus. I've done the flower from two different angles and a separate study of the stamen and a leaf. It looks a bit like an old botanical illustration.'

'Sounds great. Look, I must dash.'

'Perhaps I should have done it on cream paper. Or a sort of buff colour.'

'I'm sure it's fine as it is.'

'Parchment.'

'Mm.'

'How was your day?'

'Good, good. But I've got to get this meeting organised. I'll see you later.' The phone bangs down.

Olive holds the receiver for a moment longer then replaces it.

She makes another peanut butter sandwich. The second one doesn't taste as good as the first. The bread is stale.

The sun has set. All that remains is a single coral streak. The faintest rose blush runs along the skyline. The rest of the sky is darkened by the indigo of approaching night.

Olive stands beside the weeping canopy of rimu. Don't fade. Yet even as she thinks it the light is dimming. Rose changes to purple. Soon there will be no sign.

Her eye holds the last remnant of light but at the same time she moves deeper into the shadow of the tree. A part of her yearning for the light and another part longing for the comfort of dark. Her left hand and her right hand reaching out.

Two windows are lit up at the house, making yellow oblongs on the dark wall. Moths flutter against the glass.

Leaning on the tree Olive looks up at the dim shapes of foliage overhead, then back to the house, then up at the sky. 'Move on, move on,' she whispers. And these words spoken at random are not totally devoid of meaning.

In the half light it is easy to imagine that the top of the avocado caught silhouetted against fading pink is the upward thrusting tip of a healthy tree. It is a magnificent evening on earth.

A faint noise reaches down. Olive has heard it somewhere before. She would move away from it. A shiver passes down her back.

There is something in the air above the house. At first she cannot see a thing but the whisper sounds again. It is the sound of a hush.

And a dark shape appears above the roof. It is cloudy and moving in some way and yet solid. As she watches it splits and separates into a number of smaller shapes. Birds spin away from one another. Their flight cuts the still evening air.

They swoop beyond the roof and around then down over the garden. At this point the visibility is best. It is the flock of silver birds. There is no mistaking the precise shape and strange colour. These birds fly at nightfall. Their speed is faster than it should be. Around and around they spin. They encircle the roof of the house then dip down and soar up once more.

The evening deepens. Olive's legs are stiff now and aching. For a moment she lowers her gaze and that second is all it takes for the birds to disappear. The hush is no longer. There is nothing in the air above the house. She peers into the emptiness for some movement or sign but all is still.

Through gaps in the branches overhead the first stars of night are beginning to shine.

In the morning Olive climbs the stairs to the attic room and begins preparations for another painting.

The hibiscus branch is still upon the table but has wilted now. The flowers are flaccid. It is an unpleasant sight. Opening the window she drops the branch through. She washes her hands with a little water from the paint jar then spreads a clean sheet of paper on the table.

Without any plan in mind Olive applies paint directly onto the paper. The colours are of a similar intensity. Taking a plate to one side she mixes a variety of new shades. Red and blue blend into purple. The greens are bright.

She moves the brush one way then the other on the paper. After a while the brushstrokes take on the movement and form of a tree. It grows according to a direction of its own.

The trunk is red and the sky behind is a stirring sea of green. Verdant swirls show the air currents. At the bottom a complex pattern of roots reach into the soil. The underground part of the tree corresponds in size to the network of branches overhead. The leaves are ovals of yellow and blue.

But it's the area in front of the tree to which Olive's attention is continually drawn. The soil there is bare and soft. The colours are subtle.

With a finer brush she goes over the spot until it takes on the shape of a hollow. Ahh. A hollow in the fertile earth. Above the indentation the tree rises strong and bright.

Olive places her brush on the table and lights a cigarette. She stands there looking at her work. Although crude,

the painting is vigorous. An energy flows right through.
The soil is warm and inviting. Ah, to fling myself on the soil, she thinks. The desire is overwhelming. To lie on the soil. Cling to the breast of earth and to merge. Melt into dark loam. Ahh.

Drawing on the cigarette her gaze shifts to the window. Outside the light is bright. It reflects from iron roofs. The angles glitter beneath a flat blue sky. From all around come the faint everyday noises. There is the barely audible hum which is traffic up on the main road and the sound of starlings in the guttering of the house next door.

Against the richness of the painting it is a hard dreary reality. There is too much light. Something is wrong with the light.

Reaching out she touches the soft earth of the picture. The paint is still wet. It marks the ends of her fingertips.

Olive wanders down the stairs. She empties a small can of baked beans into a pot and puts two slices of bread into the toaster.

The time is mid-afternoon. She eats hungrily, pausing only when the plate is clean. Leaning back, she pushes it away.

Jim returns and the kitchen is warm with the smell of roasting beef. Olive serves the meat and vegetables at the table.

Taking his plate, Jim turns it, looking at it from one angle then another.

'What's the matter?' Olive says.

'Nothing.'

'Did you have a good day?'

He takes a forkful of food into his mouth. 'Stringy cow,' he says. 'You don't cook it like you used to.'

'I cook it the same way.'

'You could have fooled me.'

'Oh, I'm sorry.'

'I'll try to eat it,' he says.

Olive looks out through the window while she eats.

Jim pushes his chair back. Most of the meat is still on his plate. He moves directly from the table to the television.

'Come and watch this,' he calls through the door.
'What's that?'
'There's something good on.'
'I will later.'
'It won't be on later.'

Olive slips past. Jim pays no further attention. She quietly treads the stairs to the attic room and pulls the door shut behind.

The sun is setting over the rooftops. Flaming patches of orange scatter across the sky. It is too beautiful to watch.

Olive flicks the light switch and the red tree leaps out. Her breath sucks in and holds.

That's where I want to be. She touches the soil with tender fingers. I should be there. She imagines her body becoming one with the earth. Nurtured by it. Sinking down, sinking in.

For a moment Olive is lost to the fantasy. Her fingers press into the soil and suddenly burst through as the paper rips.

As she looks through the hole Olive's disappointment is profound. It comes not from having ruined the painting but rather from what is there.

At the bottom of the hollow there is nothing but the varnished yellow wood of the table upon which the picture lies.

CHAPTER FIVE

MICHAEL AND HIS wife Karen ring to say they will be home for the weekend.

'It's your son on the phone,' Jim calls. 'He's got some special news.'

'My son?'

'Our son. Hurry up.'

Olive takes the receiver. 'What is it?' she asks.

Michael laughs. 'Tell you on Saturday. You'll just have to wait.'

Jim leaves to meet them at the airport and Olive and the twins prepare food for a picnic.

'What's this fancy news about?' asks Heather.

'I don't know. Michael's going to make an announcement.'

'I bet she's pregnant.'

'That crossed my mind too,' Olive says. 'I don't know why.'

'We'd be aunties.'

'She'd have a terrible labour,' says Ruth.

'Yeah. Her feet are too small.'

Heather sits on the table and butters squares of white bread. Ruth spreads them with ham and chopped egg. When the sandwiches are made they sit back and begin to eat. Ruth wears a pink tracksuit and Heather's is grey. Their ankles are exactly the same.

'Leave some for the picnic,' Olive says.

'What else is there?'

'I baked all day yesterday.'

'Any cream cakes?'

'Of course.'
'Just as well.'
Ruth peels back a piece of bread and examines the filling. 'These are great. Pig sandwiches. Have one.' She waves a sandwich at Olive.
'No thanks dear, I'll wait.'
'I don't think you should.'
The twins have both stopped chewing. Olive looks away.
'You look bloody terrible,' Heather spits out.
'What's wrong?'
'You're starving yourself.'
'No I'm not.'
'Your legs look like sticks out of a concentration camp.'
Olive wraps her skirt around her thighs. 'They're not that bad.'
'Look at your eye sockets.'
'What's wrong with my eye sockets?'
'You're being irresponsible.'
'I've lost a little weight, I know.'
'Why are you doing it?'
'I'm not doing it. It's doing itself.'
'Oh bullshit,' Ruth says. 'And how come you're limping?'
'I am not. There's nothing wrong with my legs.'
'You never used to walk like that.'
'Oh.'
'Dragging along.'
'A bloody good feed would do you the world of good.' Ruth thrusts the sandwich forward.
Olive takes it and chews at a corner. Her throat is tight and the soft bread sticks like dough. She washes it down with water from the kitchen tap.
'It's a pity Annette can't be here,' she says. 'We'd have the whole family together.'
'Yeah,' Ruth replies. 'Still, that's fairly typical, isn't it?' She smiles and turns to the window. Sunlight touches the firm swell of her cheek.
Summer fruit, Olive thinks. Stone fruit. A peach. Her hair is thick and clean.
Moving away, she feels the heavy pull of her years.

The picnic spot is an acre of grass. It stretches down to a river. Tall trees dot the lawn and willows trail out over the water from the banks.

'Haven't been here for years,' Michael says. His voice seems louder than it was before.

'None of us have.'

'The river's changed,' says Olive, stepping from the car.

'No it hasn't.'

'It has.' Her eyes are fixed to the wide band of water. It appalls her. Deep and black, the river moves without a sound.

'It hasn't changed.'

'It's exactly the same.'

'Do you think so?' She shivers. 'It looks different.'

'It's definitely the same.'

Ruth and Heather practise handstands on the grass. Their bodies are agile. They balance for a long time before flipping back onto their feet.

'Where shall we eat?' Ruth calls. Her arms and legs flash by.

'By the river.' Jim takes the picnic basket.

Michael and Karen set off without looking back.

'No, no, up here!' Olive cries, but the others are already well down the slope.

The cloth is spread and the twins pile it with food. They prise the lids off plastic containers and examine the contents, rolling tomatoes and oranges on the ground.

'Hold on,' Olive says.

Heather unwraps a raisin cake. Taking a knife, she pushes it through so that a crude oblong is cut. She bites into this piece. 'Mmm.'

'Wait a minute.' Michael shifts so he is sitting on his knees. Picking up a loaf of french bread he taps it on his thigh. He looks around. His jaw is square like the twins'. Reaching for Karen's small hand he squeezes it in his own. 'Listen, everyone. We're going to have a baby.'

'Ha, ha!' the twins shout. 'Told you so!' They roll about laughing on the ground.

A tomato squashes beneath Ruth's bottom. She twists around to look at the stain. 'Jesus,' she says.

Jim takes Michael's hand and pumps it up and down. 'Well done,' he says. 'Marvellous news.'

Michael turns to his wife and kisses her on the nose.

Pushing strands of hair back off her face she smiles. 'It's due in November. On the twenty-second.'

Jim addresses Karen. 'You take good care of yourself now, won't you? Our first grandchild. We're delighted.'

'Oh yes,' she says. 'I have wheatgerm and slippery elm and everything.'

'That's lovely.'

The twins' laughter bellows across the grass. Olive is silent. The green river glides by only feet away and she cannot take her eyes from it.

'That's lovely news,' she says, and her eyes swing back to the water. It's so dark and deep. A ponga frond floats slowly by. The fern is brown and saturated. The deep water moves below. Ahh.

It takes her into a dream. After a time she stands and moves to the other side of the picnic cloth. The whole family are talking. She hasn't heard a word they have said. She sits down so the river is behind and only now is able to concentrate.

'Do you hope for a boy or a girl?' she asks.

'According to him we're having a boy, and that's all there is to it,' says Karen.

'It might be a girl.'

'No, it's going to be a boy.'

'We'll deliver it,' Ruth says. 'It's our speciality.'

'I bet.' Michael rolls his eyes. 'You two would drop the little bugger on his head. We're having a natural birth.'

'As opposed to what?'

'We don't believe in drugs and episiotomies and all that sort of interference.' Karen looks to Michael for support.

'A midwife's nightmare,' says Heather.

'We do our antenatal exercises together in the mornings before I go to work, don't we darl?' adds Michael.

'Christ.' Heather breaks off a piece of bread. 'You'd better eat something.'

Michael cuts pieces of cheese. He passes morsels of food to Karen. She picks daintily. The others eat with gusto.

Olive watches until the river calls her back. The earthy smell of water floats in the air.

'I always dream of water,' she says. 'There's nearly always water in my dreams.'

'Aren't you going to eat something?'

'Where's the tea? I'm ready for a cup of tea,' says Jim. 'You did bring the thermos?'

'It's in the basket.'

'Pass that pie over.'

'There's something about it,' Olive says.

'The pie?'

'No, the water.'

'It's bacon and egg.'

'The river, I mean the river.'

'Christ, you say some weird things.'

'What about kelp? The look of kelp in water. That's something to watch. The ocean. Ahh. We should go out to the coast one day.'

'No kelp in there, Mum,' Michael nods at the river.

'No, but there's other things.'

'Like what?'

'Deep things.'

'Yippee!' the twins shout.

'Wow,' Michael says. 'That was profound.'

'I'm being serious.'

'Ah, ha, ha!' the twins laugh. The sound rises up into sunny blue air.

After lunch the whole family take a walk. They follow a narrow path downstream. Lush plants drape down the bank and trail out in long weaving strands on the water. Jim leads the way and Olive follows at the rear. The twins bounce up and down as if they should be running and Michael and Karen walk hand in hand. It occurs to Olive to drop back. She glances at the river to one side.

'You can't see the bottom at all,' she says.

'Too deep for that.'

Trees close in and the path turns sharply to follow a bend in the river. It is darker here and enclosed.

'I might go back. I have a headache.

'Bad luck.'

'I'll go back and have a lie down. I'm sure it'll go away.'

'Good idea.'

'See you later,' the twins chorus. They continue without looking back then disappear around another bend.

Olive just stands there listening as their voices fade into the bush. There is a faint burst of laughter, then nothing.

Alone on the bank of a river, she thinks. A massive vein cuts through the land. I could drown in that. Sink and sink, never to rise again. She wants to turn away but the water keeps her there. It sweeps by without a sound.

A bird plummets from the sky and hits the surface with a splash, then vanishes below. Olive watches for its head. It emerges further downstream than she expects.

A small eel twists in its beak. The shag gulps and swallows and Olive can see its throat bulge where the eel still thrashes.

She hurries back along the path to the picnic area. Stepping from shade into the sun she stops. There is something odd about the things spread on the big red cloth. Food left from lunch is still scattered about and the wicker basket lies on its side as it was left.

She approaches warily. There is nobody to be seen and nothing appears to be missing.

Bending forward, she picks an apple up and her thumb punctures the fruit where it's spongy with rot. It drops to the ground and she's squatting to wipe her hand on the cloth. Then from the side of her eye she sees a little lump which is the last of the pâté. It is blue now. The surface is covered with fine strands of mould. A scream stifles in her throat as she throws herself back.

She stands with both hands over her throat. In half an hour the food has decayed. The french bread is grey and cracked and the remaining raisin cake is mottled with patches of white. A cream puff has collapsed into a fatty mess at the centre of the cloth. Strange colours show through the clear plastic lids of the containers.

She glances around then she's down on her knees and frantically scraping the food up. She uses two paper plates but one bends and she's tossing it aside to use her hands.

She drops the rotting things into the wicker basket. The smell is sickening and twice she turns away, choking back the vomit which rises in her throat.

She takes the basket with both hands and stumbles up the hill in search of a rubbish tin. There isn't one. She walks around the car.

A path leads upstream and away. It is narrow and overgrown. Holding the basket from her body Olive steps onto it. She pushes forward through branches which reach across. Her feet make no sound on bare earth.

A small tributary flows into the river and the path ends. She stops and puts the basket down, then lifts it up again and upends it so the contents fall into the river. The stench of decomposition rears up.

Silently, the mess sinks. The pale square of raisin cake hovers greenly, becoming fainter and fainter as it submerges and then is gone. A broken stick of french bread swells on the surface and falls apart.

Taking the basket she hurries back to the clearing. The others have not returned. The cloth is foul with stains and crumbs of rotten food. She rolls it up and sets off again. Branches lash her face but there is no time for concern about that.

Stopping at the end of the path she flings the cloth out onto the river. She washes her hands and splashes water onto her face. The bloodstain is wet like mud on her palm. She hurries away.

Voices drift up from the trees downstream and Jim and the twins appear on the opposite side of the clearing.

'Where have you been?' Ruth says.

'Nowhere.'

'The others are still coming.'

The twins look around in surprise. 'Where's the food gone?'

'A dog ate it.'

'Crappers.'

'Did it really?'

'Yes,' says Olive. Her weight shifts from one foot to the other.

'What sort of dog?'
'A water dog.'
'Here we go.'
'What is a water dog?'
'Well, a sort of labrador I think.'
'Jesus. There was a whole raisin cake,' says Jim.
'Not a whole one.'
'Half a one, then.'
'I know. It was my fault. I should have packed it all away.'
'Bloody hell.'
Michael and Karen step from the trees. 'Packed up already?' Michael says.
'Yes, it's clouding over.'
'Clouding over my arse,' says Ruth.
'You're all red in the face.'
Olive touches her cheek. The skin burns. 'It's probably hypertension,' she says.
'Ha, not you,' says Ruth.
'You're too bloody thin for that.'
'A dog ate the cake,' says Heather.
'Oh, that's great.'
Karen tilts her head and giggles. She holds one hand flat on her stomach.
From the side of her eye Olive catches a glimpse of red out on the river. The picnic cloth floats by.
'Christ!' Jim explodes. 'That's our picnic cloth!'
The family rush to the water's edge and watch as it slowly passes. Olive stays where she is further up the slope.
Don't look, don't look. Sweat prickles her brow. Her face is on fire. She turns away then looks back.
'It's not ours,' she calls. 'Ours is in the car.'
'It sure looks like ours.'
'It's not.'
'Are you sure?'
'Yes. I put it in the car. It's in the boot.'
'That's all right then,' says Jim.
Olive exhales with relief.
Far from the straggling touch of willow, in the centre

of the river where the current is strongest, the square of red floats triumphantly.

Watching it move on dark water she is lifted by a great surge of hope and joy. Everything will be all right. I'll work it out. It will be all right. Red and strong and bright. Ahh.

Laughing silently she jumps into the air.

Ruth turns and catches her in mid-leap. 'What are you doing?' she cries. 'You're a bloody nutter.'

Olive waves and shuffles her feet on the grass.

Ruth spins back to the river and Olive jumps again. Muddy heels touch the back of her woollen skirt. She laughs in her belly.

The slash of scarlet sails from sight and once more the landscape is green and brown. A bird flies upstream.

Michael and Karen leave with Jim on Monday morning. Heather and Ruth are already back at the nurses' home. The house is empty once more. The silence has been reclaimed.

The day is cold and bright. A brittle light touches all in its way. Soften down, soften down.

Olive takes a clean sheet of paper and tapes it to the table in the attic room. Turning her back to the window she lights a cigarette and stares at the expanse of white. A path comes to mind, then a forest.

Thinking of a forest she squeezes blobs of paint onto a tin plate and chooses a brush. It is a dark place she can see. Add lighter colours, she thinks, but the pigments mix as they will.

She makes a single line then thickens it in the foreground so it trails off into the distance. The path meanders across the paper and away. By itself, it is pleasing and definite.

But the forest as it takes shape is gloomy and strange. Twisted trunks rise up from the ground and branches press in over the path to meet with boughs from the other side. She tightens her hold on the brush to regulate the movement but the lines which emerge can only tangle further.

The light is blue. That which should have been sky is

the very air itself. The forest isn't safe.

Olive slides another cigarette from the packet and strikes a match. She inhales deeply.

The colour is all wrong. Taking up the brush again she paints over the trees, adding red and purple and yellow. The colours make little improvement and do nothing to alter the impression of twilight.

She outlines a person in the foreground and begins the process of filling the shape in. In time it becomes clear she is painting herself. Although the figure is intended to be upright it tilts forward as if running.

Olive completes the body and paints in the face. The features are simple. Several hours pass before she stops again and when she does she is shocked by what has come to life on the paper.

The woman's eyes are wild and staring and her lips are parted in a grimace of fear. She charges blindly down the path away from the shadowy forest. It is a primitive place.

Olive drops her brush and leaves the room. She rushes down the stairs two at a time and runs along the hall. Bursting through the front door she leaps down from the veranda and hurries along the path. She stops on the footpath and looks around. She is gasping for breath. Her heart thunders.

A small ginger cat springs from a bush and runs towards Olive. Its tail points straight up. Warm fur pushes against her ankle and it rolls over on its back. She smiles.

Across the street a tradesman whistles as he loads a ladder and planks onto the roof of his van. A yellow taxi drives by.

The world out here is as usual.

'Olive.' Jim is walking down the street. His briefcase swings from one hand and he has a rolled-up newspaper in the other.

'Hello,' she calls.

He waves the newspaper and looks at his watch.

Olive begins another painting the following day.

She colours a large sheet of paper with blue sky and dots it with drifts of white cloud. Pale ripples run across.

Her own body appears flying above the land. She has no notion where this idea has come from.

The flesh colour she mixes tends towards pink. She fills her trailing arms and legs out so they are plump and then takes a new colour for her clothing. She remembers a particular dress. It was a full-skirted one she had worn when the children were young. She whips the paint so it seems the garment billows in the wind. It has a wide collar and padded shoulders and a narrow yellow belt.

Down below, the blue paint has run into a darker shadow. The shape is suggestive of land. She goes over it, darkening the discoloration until it has changed to become a landscape of rolling hills. The contours stretch to a certain point and then end in a long curve of coast. She paints the sea and a pale line which is the horizon.

At the bottom she writes 'Self-portrait' with a pencil and then adds a question mark. I'm not sure. With pins she attaches it to the wall next to the picture of herself on the forest path. The paint still glistens wet in places.

Olive is both excited and exhausted by the painting and she lies down on the floor. She wants to look at it and at the same time look away. Her eyes are stuck regardless. She watches reflections dull as the paint dries.

In time sleep comes to claim her. The darkness descends.

Eventually something reaches in. She opens one eye then the other. Jim stands at the attic room door.

Horrified, he leans there looking down. 'What the hell is the matter?'

'Ahh.'

'Olive.'

She stretches out. 'I had a sleep.'

'Jesus. On the floor?'

'It's quite warm.' Scrambling to her feet Olive clutches her cardigan across her chest in confusion. One thumb pushes into a buttonhole and she's pulling it out.

Jim slowly enters the room. He looks from one side to the other. 'Someone's been smoking in here,' he says.

'Well.'

'The air stinks of it.'

'Yes.'

'Who's been smoking?'
'Nobody has been here.'
He looks at the paintings. 'Jesus Christ,' he says.
'Don't you like them?' Olive pulls the cardigan tighter.
'Like them? How could I possibly like them?'
'Oh.'
'Are they yours?'
'Yes. I did that today.' She points and her hand goes back over her chest.
'It's dreadful,' he says. 'Why do stuff like this when you can paint properly?' He waves his arm at the hibiscus painting where it lies on the floor.
Olive looks at the red on green and the delicate stamen. She bursts into tears.
Jim stares in disbelief. 'What? What is it?'
She slides down the wall until she is sitting with her head on her knees. Tears splash on the wooden floor.
'And what's this?'
Olive makes no move and now he is beside her. He pushes her head back. The ashtray filled with cigarette butts is in his hand.
'Whose are they?'
'Mine,' she sobs.
'Yours?'
'Yes.'
'But Olive, you don't smoke!'
'I just had a few.'
'A few! There's six in here. Seven. Why?'
She cries silently. Tears well up in her eyes so she can't see. 'I don't know.'
'What do you mean, you don't know? Christ.'
'Someone left a packet in the house and I smoked them.'
'But why?'
Olive shrugs. Her shoulders sink again.
'Are there any left?'
'No.'
'It's a disgusting habit. You've no call to smoke. It doesn't make sense.'
'I know.'
'And that. What about that? I don't understand.'

Olive stares at the marks her tears have made on the dry wooden floor. One has splashed out into a long shape. It looks like a boat. A thin vessel with a pointed prow and water churning behind. The other tears are islands.

'The painting, Olive. The woman in the trees. How could you paint something like that? Is it supposed to be you? I sincerely hope not.'

'What's wrong with it?'

'It's horrific.'

'I know. But it's important.'

'Important? How?'

'I don't know. I can't explain. But I do know it's important.'

'It's psychotic,' he says.

'No, no, it's important. It is. They're opposites. The pictures are opposites. Flying, and look at the other one. What about the stuff in between?'

'What stuff in between?'

'The path in between.'

'You're making absolutely no sense at all.'

'I have to know which way to go.'

'Go where?'

'Psychotic. You said it's psychotic.' Olive drops to the floor. Pain shoots through her left hip. She curls on her side. 'Psychotic. They called her that.'

'Who?'

'Mummy.'

'Get up!' he shouts.

'I can't.'

'Get up!'

'Don't shout at me like that.'

'Please, Olive. You look terrible lying on the floor.'

Olive rises onto one elbow. It takes all her energy.

'I'm not knocking you, you know.' Jim picks the hibiscus painting up and waves it savagely. 'You've got real talent. We employ graphic artists who can't produce stuff like this. I just think you should stick with this sort of thing.'

'What's the point? I might as well take a photograph.'

'Nonsense. There's a lot of skill involved in painting realistically.'

'It's meaningless to me. I want to know about the stuff the camera doesn't catch. The important things.'

'Look, perhaps psychotic was a bit strong, love. But that painting is very tortured and unpleasant. I think you're making yourself very, very unhappy. You know that, don't you?'

Olive shuts her eyes. 'Yes,' she says. 'Yes, yes, yes. I suppose you're right.'

They descend the stairs and Olive goes into the kitchen. Blindly she chops three large onions for dinner.

Jim changes from his suit into corduroy trousers and a jersey. 'I'm ready to eat,' he calls from the bedroom.

'It won't be done for a wee while yet.'

'I see.'

'I've got the meat on. I've made a cup of tea.'

'Yes, I'll have a cup of tea.'

'Come and get it then.'

His head appears around the door. 'David's in trouble again.'

'What is it now?'

'A drug conviction. He's in hospital here in Auckland.'

'Hospital. What's wrong?'

'A psychiatric hospital.'

'Oh, poor David!'

'Bugger David. Poor Jean, I should think.'

'Your sister's children are always in trouble.'

'It's hard for her being a widow. Being on her own.'

'Yes, I know. Shall I pour your tea?'

'If you would.'

A hot stream of tea gushes from the teapot. A dribble runs down the spout, soaking into the tea-cosy. The yellow wool is stained brown at this point. Olive looks away from the discoloration.

'Six o'clock and it's dark,' she says. 'Winter's here.'

'When it's dark at five o'clock in the evening that's when it's winter.'

'How did you hear about David?'

'Jean rang me at work.'

'She rang you at work?'

'Yes, why not?'
'Is it serious?'
'Sounds as if it could be. She's coming up to Auckland.'
'The poor boy. He's so young. It's awful. He must be feeling terrible.'
'He's old enough to know better. Jean will be staying here with us.'
'Oh.'
Jim stirs sugar into his tea and drops the spoon on his saucer. 'I'm drinking my tea in the other room,' he says. 'Is there any cake?'
'No. I'm sorry.'
'Well.'
Olive follows him into the lounge. A circle of light radiates from the standard lamp. The perimeters of the room are shadowy. Jim takes a seat within the warm glow.
'When will she come?'
'Tomorrow afternoon.'
'Tomorrow. That soon?'
'She wants to be able to visit David at the hospital.'
'Oh.'
'Oh what?'
'I don't know.'
'You'd want to be nearby if one of our kids was in trouble, wouldn't you?'
'Yes, of course.'
'Well then.' He flicks the front page of the newspaper. 'Look at this. Two people jumped off the harbour bridge last night. A man and a woman.'
'Two people together or two people separately?'
'Two people together but they weren't a married couple. Their surnames aren't the same.'
'They must have loved each other very much.'
'Not necessarily. Perhaps they couldn't stand each other. How would you know?'
'Did they die?'
'They certainly did.' Jim turns the page and scans both sides.
'Ahh. I'm sure they must have loved each other. Does it say whether they jumped facing out to sea or facing

up the harbour?'

'What's that?' Jim mumbles.

'The moon was yellow last night. I noticed it. I hope they jumped facing out to sea. I could imagine dying then, but not facing inland. It's too dark up the harbour.'

'A woman and a child drowned on the west coast today as well. The woman went in to rescue the child. They haven't recovered the bodies.'

Looking to the ocean with a full moon rising. Olive jumps to her feet. 'I have to peel the potatoes,' she says. 'There's a casserole in the oven.'

'Good show. It wasn't even her child. It was the neighbours' son.'

Olive slams the door.

'A five-year-old boy!' he calls.

She goes out through the back door and down into the dark garden. Shining a torch over the vegetable patch she bends forward and cuts firm stalks of silverbeet for the meal.

In the hot light of the kitchen Olive discovers she has chosen older leaves. Although crisp to the touch some of them are yellow. On one crinkled leaf a small snail glides, leaving a bumpy trail of silver.

Olive touches the snail's shell tenderly and the translucent stalks of its eyes withdraw. After a moment they emerge again and it continues easily on its way.

Olive leaves the breakfast dishes and hurries upstairs with a jar of water. She smooths a fresh piece of paper on the table and squeezes paint onto a plate. The colours are a random selection. Red and green glisten next to each other. Burnt sienna and umber are less intense.

Standing there looking at the blank paper she slips into a dream. Nothing comes. No ideas emerge. After a while she sits down on the floor. Her eyes are fixed on the window.

An hour passes. At ten o'clock she jumps up and hurries down the stairs. She leaves the house and walks up the hill to the dairy.

Boxes of green bananas and bags of potatoes and onions

are stacked up at the door. She steps through.

'A packet of Benson and Hedges, please,' she says.

The shopkeeper passes them without comment.

'And a box of matches, please.'

He pushes the smaller box over the counter.

On the footpath outside she strips the cellophane away and places the dry end of a cigarette between her lips.

The sun is swollen and white. It is a cold day. A metal bread sign bangs in the breeze.

Olive wanders along the road for a short distance, then doubles back and makes her way down the hill. Cream and white villas line both sides of the road. Some of the houses have been renovated recently and the colours are brighter and more varied. She smokes the cigarette as she walks. White points of light glitter on the harbour below.

A man crosses the road in front and approaches a woman on the footpath. She wears a blue sweatshirt and her pregnant belly bulges, stretching the tight cloth. The woman lifts her arms and he passes her a large green watermelon.

Olive slows. For a moment they look to her. Both the man and the woman have one squinting eye. His is on the left and hers is on the right.

Holding the melon against the hard swell of her body the woman moves away. She leans back further to compensate for the additional weight.

It seems no coincidence that they part without exchanging a word.

In the attic room Olive runs a finger over the mounds of paint where they have dried on the tin plate. Taking several tubes she squeezes fresh pigment out.

Coating the brush with green paint she runs it in a large circle on the paper. Filling the circle in, she shades it so the shape becomes a melon. A green watermelon floats against a backdrop of dark space. Before the deep background colour has dried, Olive dots the area with pinpricks of white paint. They are the stars. In places the colours smear together. She works rapidly and without care.

Jean will be coming soon. And there will be no more time in the attic room. Panic loosens her hand.

Rinsing the brush she loads it with green again. Emerald paint slaps onto the paper. She spreads it with broad sweeps of the brush.

The painting isn't working. It is simply a green blob in space. A green rock or spinning dinner plate. The mass of colour takes on nothing to distinguish it as a water-melon.

Take care, she thinks. Take care.

She scrapes at the paint and adds a darker colour so the skin will be mottled. The pigments mix and become muddy on the paper.

The doorbell sounds downstairs. Snatching the painting up Olive rips it in half and folds the pieces sticky sides together.

Jean stands on the front veranda. She wears a tight woollen suit and the scarf at her throat is the same vivid pink as her lipstick and fingernails. She smiles and offers a powdered cheek to be kissed.

Olive hesitates. For a moment she just stands there, then she is smiling. 'Oh Jean,' she says. 'Come in.'

She busies herself at the kitchen bench, filling the electric kettle for tea and arranging biscuits on a plate. 'I'm sorry to hear about David.'

'Silly boy he is.' Jean lowers herself elegantly onto a chair. 'Olive,' she says. 'You look absolutely terrible.'

Olive fusses with the cups and saucers and pours milk from a bottle into a jug. 'I was going to change and tidy up a bit before you came. But I wasn't exactly sure when you were due.'

'Oh it doesn't matter. I don't mean to be rude, you know that. But you do just look dreadful.'

'I've lost a bit of weight.'

'You're skin and bones.' Jean plucks at the loose fabric in the seat of Olive's trousers. 'You used to fill these trousers.'

'They were never tight.'

'They look like jodhpurs.'

'Did you fly up today?' Olive asks.

'Yes, I did. My flight was direct.'
'Lovely.'
'I came without warning, of course, so I'm not as well prepared as I'd like to be. But well what can you do about it?'
'That's right.'
Jean raises her manicured hands and smiles. 'Your hair needs a bit of attention. What sort of conditioner have you been using?'
'Egg,' Olive says.

CHAPTER SIX

A STORM BLOWS up during the night. Wind lashes rain against the windows and bends the bamboo. Stalks of it scratch on the side of the house.

Olive is unable to sleep for the noise. In bed beside her, Jim is undisturbed. One arm is folded across his chest and the other is flung out over the bedding. His hands are open.

Olive steps from the bed. Pulling a jacket over her nightdress she goes down the hall to the guest room. She peers through the door. Details are obscure in the dark. Jean's breath is deep and even.

Walking back up the hall, she makes her way blindly to the back door. It leaps open to a blast of cold air and she moves out onto the steps.

The garden is black and the shapes of trees are barely separable from the sky but their movement is evident. Tall trees on the boundary thrash and heave in the gale and the air is sharp with the creaking of straining boughs.

Wrapping the jacket tight around her, Olive shivers. For a split second the whole garden is illuminated by a great flash of lightning. The sad avocado is caught by a clear blue light. It bends away from the south. Lengths of branch are stripped bare and leaves whip about in tatters. The strange light lends the wood of the tree the pliancy of skin. In its plight the avocado is caught and frozen. A thin woman leans her ravaged back to the squall. Ahh.

Instantly the garden is black again but the picture is indelible.

An enormous boom of thunder shakes the house. The steps shiver beneath Olive's feet. She clings on to the handrail.

Flying iron crashes and the wind blows the sound up from the bottom of the street. It wails and cracks. A new burst of thunder roars again.

Olive moves back inside the house. She locks the door and tiptoes through to the attic stairway. She rushes up in the dark.

A little light enters the attic room window. Sitting with her back against the wall she smokes cigarettes and waits for the slow dawn. Time stretches on.

With the pale grey wash of sunrise comes the first break in the storm. Rain slows to a patter on the windows and the howling wind fades then is still.

The sky lightens and gradually objects in the room take on shape and then detail. The bird marks stand out keenly on the wooden sill.

Olive stabs out her last cigarette and rises to her feet. She creeps down the stairs and into the bathroom.

She brushes her teeth in the shower. Hot water sprays over her aching head and face. Her eyes are shut.

The bathroom door opens and Jim comes in. 'You're up early,' he says.

She runs one hand over her forehead, pushing back wet strands of hair. 'No earlier than usual.'

Jim wipes the mirror with a towel and studies his reflection. The glass mists over again immediately. 'I'm starving.'

'I'll do bacon and eggs.' Olive steps from the shower and wraps a towel tightly around her shoulders.

Jim adjusts his tie. 'Make sure the eggs are soft in the middle. They've been like pebbles lately.'

Olive sets the pan on the stove and puts coffee on to boil.

'You've washed your hair,' Jim says. 'You shouldn't wash your hair on a morning like this. You'll catch a cold. It's starting to rain out there.'

'Starting to rain. It's been raining all night.'

'Has it?'

'There was a terrible storm.'

'Last night?'

'The house rattled all night. The thunder was terrible.'

'Didn't hear a thing.'

'I hope Jean slept well.'

'Is she awake yet?' Jim pulls a chair in at the table.

Olive slides his plate across. 'No, she's asleep still.'

'This egg's not bad,' he says, poking at the yolk with his knife. 'But I prefer them softer in the middle. They're best cooked until the white is set and the yolk is sealed but still runny inside. Hard eggs give me indigestion.'

Taking an umbrella, Olive slips out through the back door. She shuts it quietly behind and makes her way down the garden path to the orchard. The rain has softened down to mist.

A broken branch gleams white in fallen leaves at the foot of the avocado. Grinding her teeth, she turns away.

A pale bloom lightens the ground beneath the plum tree. Hundreds of white petals lie scattered on the grass. The branches overhead are naked but the bruised petals are all about.

Dropping the umbrella, Olive bends over. She collects the delicate petals and plasters them onto the palm of her hand so the bloodstain is covered. It shows faintly through the film of damp petals.

She adds another layer and smooths it down. Under the poultice the blemish disappears.

'Olive!' Jim calls from the back door. 'For Christ's sake, you're getting wet!'

'I'm coming.'

She walks up the path.

'There's no debris in the garden,' Jim says. 'It can't have been that much of a storm.'

'It was. I found petals under the plum tree.' Olive cups her hand behind her back and moves sideways through the door.

'It had a false spring.'

'When?'

'Last week sometime. There was blossom on the plum.'

'There can't have been.'

'Why not?'

'I didn't see it.'

'I mentioned it to you at the time,' Jim says.

'No, I'm sure you didn't.'
'It's happened before. Blossom in the winter.'
'I know. But imagine not noticing something like that!' Olive shouts.
'Jesus. Take it easy.'
'That I shouldn't notice!'
'Well, what of it?'
Olive pours coffee and gulps the scalding liquid. It burns the end of her tongue.
'You don't drink black coffee.'
'I don't care.'
Frowning, Jim steps back. 'What are you and Jean going to do today?'
'I don't know. I imagine she'll want to visit David at the hospital.'
'Of course. Tell her to take the car. If you'll drive me into work this morning I'll bus home.' Jim lifts his jacket from the back of the chair.
'I'll get my bag.'
In the bedroom, Olive shakes her hand over the unmade bed and wet petals fall off in clumps. The bloodstain gleams darkly once more.
Olive unlocks the car and opens the passenger door from the inside for Jim. She backs slowly out of the garage and swings around onto the street.
Traffic is heavy on the main road. She drives the car through tender rain into the city.
'Have a nice day with Jean.' The door clicks open and he's stepping onto the kerb. His black umbrella glides open.
A man in a long grey coat pushes forward. Jim and the man shake hands and laugh.
Olive pulls out into a slow stream of cars. She drives straight home.
The house is quiet. Olive goes into the bedroom and searches through the bed for the plum petals. They are brown and pulpy now and stuck to the blankets and sheets.
As she picks them off they squash between her fingers.
Jean is still asleep.

Olive walks up the hill in the rain. At the counter of the

corner dairy the shopkeeper stands reading the morning paper. He looks up and nods as she enters the shop.

'Nasty morning out there,' he says.

'At least the wind has stopped.'

'I didn't notice it blowing.'

'It was a terrible storm.'

He folds the newspaper. His hand runs over the crease. 'When was that, then?'

'The storm in the night.'

'Oh,' he says. 'First I knew about it.'

'There was a dreadful storm in the night.'

'Fancy that. We must have slept through it. The wife didn't mention a thing. What can I do for you today?'

'I've never heard such loud thunder,' Olive says.

'Is that right?'

'And the wind was terrible.'

'Fancy.'

'I want to buy some eggs, please.'

The shopkeeper takes a box of eggs and puts them on the counter.

'I'd rather have free-range, please.'

'Can't get them,' he says. 'This is all there is.'

'They'll be fine. My husband complains that I cook his eggs too hard.'

The man laughs and strokes his moustache. 'You can come and cook my eggs any time,' he says. 'My wife cooks them like slush so they run around on the plate. If there's one thing I hate it's eggs like slush. For eighteen years we've been married and she still serves me eggs like slush. "Beverly," I say, "I can't eat these eggs." And do you know what she says?'

'What?'

'She says, "I thought you liked them like that, dear. I thought you liked them runny, dear."' He mimics a woman's voice.

'And I want some cigarettes, please.'

'Nice and soft in the middle,' he pouts.

'Benson and Hedges, please.'

He slaps them on the counter.

Olive takes the money from her purse and puts the

eggs and cigarettes into her bag. Halfway to the door she stops.

'Forgotten something?'

'Is it possible to buy a watermelon?' she asks. 'At this time of year?'

'Now?'

'Yes. A watermelon.'

'I don't have any, I'm afraid.'

'No, but can they be bought?'

'Yeah, I've seen them at the market.'

'Big green ones?'

'Long green ones, round green ones. All sorts,' he says.

'Where do they grow in winter?'

'Tonga. They ship them down from Tonga.'

'Ah, I see. Thank you.' Olive tucks her bag under the flap of her coat and steps out into the rain.

Jean is pouring coffee in the kitchen. 'Hello there,' she says. 'Where have you been?'

'Up to the shop to buy some eggs.'

"There's a wet patch on your skirt.'

'I walked.'

'In the rain?'

'Yes. Let me cook you some breakfast.'

'No thanks.' Jean smooths her dressing gown over her hips. 'Unlike some people, I have to watch my weight.'

'Will you visit David today? Jim's left the car.'

Jean traces a line of water down the window with her fingernail. 'Not today,' she says. 'I want to wear my tan stilettos and the heels will stick into the lawn at the hospital. I'll have to leave it for a finer day, I'm afraid.'

'Ah, I see.'

'Let's go shopping. Let's buy you some clothes that actually fit.'

'I don't know about that.'

'You need to smarten yourself up for Jim. If you're going to be a beanstalk you might as well be a well-dressed one.'

'I don't really want to go to town.'

'It will cheer you up,' Jean announces.

'I don't need cheering up.'

'You could have fooled me. Besides, I have to go to town. I need a manicure.'

'Look.' Olive says. 'Oh look! The rain has stopped!'

The city is damp and hushed. Jean's heels click up and down the footpaths between dress shops and Olive follows behind.

'Come on,' Jean says stepping through a doorway. 'We're getting nowhere.'

'I like this one,' Olive says finally. She holds a jacket out.

'But it's black.'

'I like it. I like the cut.'

'Every single thing you've expressed any interest in has been black.'

'Yes.'

'Buff and camel are the season's colours.'

'What's wrong with black?'

'You're undernourished and colourless. You'd look absolutely terrible in black.'

'I've never worn it.'

'No, and I don't think you should start now. Something with a bit of warmth.' She holds a beige jacket against Olive.

'Yes, it's very nice.'

'Buy it then.'

'Yes, all right. I'll take this one.'

'This skirt will match.'

'Yes, I'll buy that too.'

The shop assistant pops forward from behind a rack of dresses. 'A lovely choice,' she says. 'You have good taste. There's a cream silk blouse here. It matches perfectly. What do you think?'

'Yes, that's very nice. I'll take it. Would you wrap them up, please.'

'What size is it for the blouse?'

'That one you've got there. That one will do.'

'You'd better try them on,' hisses Jean.

'I don't need to. I'll write the cheque out.'

'They mightn't fit!'

'They'll be fine.'
'How do you know they will?'
Stepping into the dressing room, Olive slams the door. She sits on a chair with the garments across her lap and stares into the mirror.
The faint wail of a fire-engine sounds from outside. It grows louder and louder then passes and fades into the distance.
'Fool, fool!' she mouths. A flushed and wary face stares back. Don't even know who you are, she thinks. A single tear wells in one eye and rolls down her cheek. She watches the descent. It falls onto the blouse in her hand.
The mark it leaves on the silk is precisely the shape of a bird in flight. A small bird with the split tail of a swallow.
'Oh Christ!' Olive whispers. She pushes her face into the silk and feels it cool on her blazing skin. For a moment she holds it then pulls back.
Standing up, she folds the blouse to hide the mark then pushes the changing room door.
'I'll take them,' she says.
Jean looks up in surprise. 'Did you try them on?'
'Yes.'
'You didn't show me.'
'I'll show you at home.'
'How did they look?'
'Fine.'
'Oh good.'
Olive places the garments on the counter. The shop assistant rearranges the blouse and the stain is visible.
'It's beautiful silk,' Jean says.
Neither she nor the shop assistant appear to notice the mark. It stands out dark and tattoo-neat. A small bird in climbing flight.
Olive writes the cheque and throws it down. Taking the parcel she hurries to the door. The heat spreads down her back.
'Slow down,' Jean says. 'You need trousers too.'
'This is enough for today.'
'It's only eleven o'clock!'

'I don't find it easy.'
'Don't find what easy?'
'Shopping.'
'Nonsense,' Jean says. 'It's fun.'
'It brings me out in a sweat. My armpits are wet.'
'Any good deodorant will solve that problem. Two pairs of trousers you need at least. You look dreadful in those baggy things you wear.'
They stand in the shop doorway looking out.
A stream of muddy water surges in the gutter. A small child darts across the footpath and steps down into the water. It flows up around his calves and he looks down and blinks. His blue overalls deepen to black where the fabric saturates.
A woman lifts him by one arm and sets him back on the footpath. A gauze bandage binds one leg beneath her stocking. Nylon stretches over white cotton. It has the look of the raised band around the middle of an earthworm.
Olive thinks of soil. In this canyon of concrete and steel the association is agreeable.
The woman pokes him under the chin and laughs and the child laughs back. His front teeth protrude.
'Feet,' he says gaily. 'Feet feet feet.'
His wet trouser legs slap together and his shoes squelch as he follows her away. Olive turns her ears to the tiny sounds until they are drowned by traffic on the street.
'Olive!'
'Oh.'
'You've not heard a single word I said,' Jean says. 'Have you?'
'Oh, I'm sorry.'
'I'll get my nails done and we'll meet in an hour.'
'Fine. Did you see that child?'
'The brat in the gutter?'
'He was lovely. He reminded me of my brother when he was little.'
'I'd have given him a jolly good smack. Those shoes will be ruined. They were good ones too.'
'My brother was a beautiful child. I was six years older than him and when my mother went into hospital I had

to take care of him.'

'I thought he died.'

'He died on his eighteenth birthday. He was a young man. He was only fifteen months old when Mum went away. He had little corduroy pants. I used to wash them in the sink and put them on the hedge to dry.'

'It was different in those days.'

'It was a boxthorn hedge,' Olive says. 'That child just then reminded me of William when he was small. He had a sort of high forehead. I used to think Michael had the same sort of look but Jim said that Michael's looks come from your side of the family and I guess he was right. He had a high forehead and these bright eyes. And his teeth were forward.'

'Whose teeth were?'

'My brother's. I used to paint an egg for him at Easter. After he was asleep at night I'd sit up and paint a hard-boiled egg at the kitchen table. I was only seven when she went away. Sometimes I made a spotted egg and when I was a bit older I used to paint a whole little scene.'

'On an egg?'

'Yes, an egg.'

'Olive, I don't know about you but I'm freezing. It's too cold to stand still.'

'Yes, it is cold. I'll see you in an hour then.'

'Twelve-fifteen. Don't forget.' Jean sails off on her heels.

Olive fumbles in her bag for a cigarette. Placing it between her lips she lights it and pushes the spent match back into the box. She wanders along watching people as they pass.

Outside of her awareness she has made her way to the print shop. She stands on the footpath until the cigarette is finished and then enters. The same man sits at a desk.

'Have you anything of Alan Rogers?' she asks.

'He's dead.'

'Yes, I know. I bought a print of his. "Calm before the storm".'

'I do recall the picture. Very fine. It was the last.'

'There was a tree. A winter tree.'

'Indeed there was. An exquisite print, an oak, but I'm

afraid it's sold.' The man shrugs and his bald head shines. He looks down at a piece of paper on the desk.

'Is there anything else?'

'I'm afraid not. I've sold a lot of his work over the years but that's it now.'

'He did trees and storms,' Olive says. 'Did he ever do birds or eggs?'

'Birds or eggs?' The man tilts his head and frowns. 'No, nothing like that.'

'Ah.'

'He did trees and rivers and storms. That type of thing.'

'Ahh. Rivers. Deep rivers?'

'I suppose so.'

'I see.'

'Well, any sort really. I don't know that he only did deep ones.'

'Shallow ones too?'

'We do have some very nice bird prints by other artists,' the man says. 'Would you like to see some?'

'No, it's all right, thank you. I was just wondering — you know — whether he ever did eggs or birds.

'Perhaps you're thinking of someone else.'

'Perhaps I am. Thank you.'

She walks out but stops to look back at the shop window. Three potted-geranium prints stand on display. The orange of the blooms is hard and plastic on a surface of blue tiles. There is not a trace of softness in the flowers.

She lights another cigarette.

Arriving early at the coffee shop Olive buys a pot of tea and a triangle of cake and claims a table near the door.

An old man comes in and looks the cakes and sandwiches up and down behind their plastic covers. His jacket is shiny with age and the cuffs of his trousers are threadbare.

Olive's eyes are upon his hands. The skin on the back of his hands is mottled and brown with liver spots.

Walking up and down in front of the counter his hands push into his pockets and out again. He unzips a small black purse and fumbles with his change. Two young women queuing behind the man sigh impatiently and step in front.

Olive pours a cup of tea and adds milk. Turning to one side she looks out the window.

The sight of the old man counting change at the cake counter is distressing. His shoes are huge and old and they knock on the floor. Each moment he spends deciding what to buy is an agony of sadness.

High up between the slab sides of multi-storied buildings a small patch of sky shows. It is the same drab grey of the buildings, but as Olive watches a soft finger of pink cloud crosses.

Pink moving on grey. It is the only thing of beauty to be seen.

Although there is beauty of a sort in the knotted hands of the old man. But there is a sadness also and it is greater.

Still he counts his change. Taking a plate he puts it on a tray and surveys the food again. Twice he reaches out and withdraws. His hand is a twisted bird. It hangs at his side. Finally he takes a pikelet with jam.

Olive pushes her plate of cake aside and lights a cigarette. At the next table the two young women compare fingernails.

'"Coral island" this polish is called,' one of them says, spreading her fingers.

'You should try my cuticle remover,' her friends says. 'It's a dream.'

The pink cloud weakens and drifts apart.

Jean appears at the coffee shop door. Olive furtively stabs her cigarette out and then waves.

Jean hurries over. 'I'm so excited,' she says. 'They did such a good job. Look.' Her nails are immaculately pointed and coloured.

'That's lovely.'

'I'll grab a coffee. Back in a minute.'

'Coral Island,' Olive cries in her head. A blood moon in Coral Island.

The old man takes the last bite of his pikelet and chews slowly. Red jam spots his chin and as his jaw moves the jam runs down. It leaves a faint trail. He wipes it with the back of his hand and rubs his hand with a handkerchief. His eyes look straight ahead.

'Aren't you going to eat that piece of cake?' Jean asks.
'No, I don't feel like it.'
'There's a dirty ashtray on the table. How disgusting!'
'I'll move it over here.' Olive pushes it onto an empty table alongside.
'Poor service. Very poor. A filthy ashtray in front of you when you're trying to eat is not the most pleasant thing in the world.' Jean smiles and her teeth sink into a sandwich. 'Did you buy any trousers?'
'No.'
'After lunch?'
'Another day.'
'Are you sure you don't want that cake?'
'Absolutely.'
'Well,' Jean says. 'Waste not, want not.' She pulls the plate towards her across the table.
The old man seems to have gone to sleep. His head has dropped onto his chest and his eyes are closed.
As his shoulders rise and fall his cup of tea grows cold.
The sight of Jean's nails, scarlet against the rich chocolate of the cake, makes Olive want to cry.

After dinner, Jim lights a fire in the lounge.
That's about the only thing these old houses are good for,' Jean says. 'Fireplaces.'
The orange flames are squat at first but as the kindling catches they rise up and bend towards the chimney. In one place the fire burns violet but then that too changes to orange.
'What did this house feel like when you were a child?' Olive asks.
'How do you mean?' Jean says.
'It must have been different. How did it feel?'
'The same as it does now, I suppose. It's the same house.'
'You're always asking that question,' Jim says.
'I keep asking it because you don't seem to understand what I mean.'
'You've redecorated of course,' says Jean. 'Remember that dreadful coal range that used to be in the kitchen, Jim?'

'I do.'

'It would drive me crazy, a thing like that.'

Olive rises to her feet. 'I'll get supper.'

'Try your new clothes on,' Jean says. 'Show us what they look like on.'

'I'll get supper first.'

'No, do it now. You said you would after dinner. Go on. I'll get the tea organised.'

Olive unwraps the parcel in the bedroom. The silk blouse spills out on the bed. Turning it to the light she searches for the bird mark. It has gone. The tear has dried. No trace of any such mark remains.

Without unbuttoning the blouse she slips it over her head. The garment is too large. The sleeves end at the last joint of her fingers and it gapes at her throat. The jacket also is oversized and the skirt swims on her waist.

Jean calls at the door and the handle turns. She steps into the room. 'My God, Olive!' she shrieks. 'They don't fit at all!'

Olive sits on the bed plucking at a cuff.

'You can't wear those clothes, they're massive! You look dreadful!'

'Yes.'

'What ever possessed you to buy them? They're sizes too big. Lift up the jacket! Look at that waist band! You said they looked good.'

'They looked different in the dressing room.'

Jean nods her head slowly. 'They certainly must have,' she says.

'It's those neon lights. They make things look different.'

'You can't blame the lights for this.'

'No.' Olive stands up and unzips the skirt. It falls to the floor and she steps from it. She takes the other things off and pulls her dressing-gown tight around the middle.

'I don't understand how you could have bought them. You should have showed me in the shop.'

'Yes.'

'We can only hope the store will change them.' Jean takes the clothes up and drapes them on a hanger. 'Back to town tomorrow,' she says, one hand is on her hip. 'And

we'll try again.'
'How did you manage it?' Jim says.
Olive stares gloomily into the fire. 'I don't know.'
'You're pretty thin.'
'So everyone keeps telling me.'
'Well, you must buy accordingly.'
'Yes.'
'I trust the shop will change them.'
'Don't worry,' Jean says. 'I'll see that they do.'
Olive pours the tea and passes a plate of cheese and crackers. When the teapot is empty she goes out to the kitchen and fills the electric kettle.
The evening newspaper is spread on the kitchen table. She stands there reading it while the water boils. Near the bottom of the front page a small headline stands out. 'Storm in the night.'
Snatching the paper she rushes back into the lounge. The television is on. Jim and Jean glance up.
'Look! It's here in the paper!'
'What is?'
'The storm in the night.'
'Oh,' says Jean. 'This is one of my favourite programmes. Come and watch it.'
'Have you got that tea?' asks Jim.
'The kettle's on. I'll get it in a minute. Listen to this. "Gale force winds lashed the city last night damaging power lines in west Auckland and causing surface flooding in many areas."'
Jean laughs. 'Look, you must watch this. It's hilarious.'
On television an old lady is sprayed with water flung up from the wheels of a passing bus. She shakes her fist and throws apples onto the street.
'Do you remember me telling you there was a storm in the night?'
'Yes,' says Jim.
'But you didn't hear it?'
'No, I didn't.'
'And you didn't either?'
'What's that?' says Jean.
'You weren't aware of the storm last night?'

'No, I slept like a log.' Her eyes turn back to the television.

'And the man at the dairy. I mentioned it to him and he didn't know there'd been a storm either.'

'Ha ha ha.' Jim and Jean stare at the television. 'Ha ha ha,' they laugh.

'Well, it's here in the paper. "Gale force winds," etcetera etcetera.'

'What's the matter?' asks Jim.

'Nothing is. I was just beginning to wonder if I'd imagined it or something. That's all.'

'Ha ha ha,' they laugh. The old woman struggles to open a gate and dances with rage. Oranges bounce from her bag and roll onto the street while her bony legs flash up and down.

Olive gathers cups and saucers and puts them on the tray. 'I'll get the tea.'

Stopping at the door she looks back. Jim and Jean and the fire and the television form a circle in the room. On one side the fire glows orange and on the other side the television is blue. The colours are opposites but are bound together by the warm light of the standard lamp. The boundary of light coincides with the boundary of the circle.

Jim and Jean laugh and their eyes shut sleepily. They have the same square jaw and high cheek-bones but Jean's features are as feminine as his are male. A man and a woman.

There is no way into this circle. It is balanced in every sense.

Outside the glow of light on a low table a china vase contains the last of the chrysanthemums. They are yellow and dusty now and the colour has faded.

Ah yes, Olive thinks. There I am.

'I should have thrown those chrysanthemums out!' she cries.

A petal detaches and drifts down onto the glass of the table top. It lies curved above its own reflection.

'They're finished. I should have thrown them out. But it's all right, I'll pick some fresh ones tomorrow and they will be lovely.'

Jim and Jean are engrossed in the programme and don't

register her words.

'I'm hurting,' she says and the blood rushes to her face.

Neither of them move. 'Ha ha ha,' they laugh.

'It was a terrible storm,' Olive says and her eyes are hot with tears. 'It really was. It was. It says so in the paper.'

Spinning around, she leaves the room. In the kitchen Olive discovers the flowers aren't old at all but are poorly arranged and the stalks are uneven in length. Their shabby attitude comes from being lopsided in the vase rather than from age.

Nevertheless she throws them out from the back porch into the garden. A frail moon glitters in an ebony sky. Dark up the harbour tonight, she thinks.

Flying through the air the chrysanthemums cut a pale arc in the night and are gone.

CHAPTER SEVEN

THERE ARE NO more chrysanthemums. The plants are stringy now and the leaves are pale with the white bloom of age.

Olive cuts them back and makes a neat pile of the trimmings. Nothing remains but a severed row of stalks.

She turns the soil along the garden wall with the hoe and plants bulbs for the spring. Amongst the pruned chrysanthemums she puts in freesias and further back a number of irises. The positions are random for an informal effect.

She clears the cornflower bed and digs it over for the daffodils. The earth is cold now and the rising scent is raw. She makes depressions with her hands.

'Keep warm,' she says. 'Keep warm.' She pats the bulbs down in frosty soil.

There is a meagre warmth where the morning sun touches the back of her neck. In their plastic gloves her fingers are numb. She stops and wriggles them about. Pins-and-needles shoot through her left hand. There is a hush in the garden.

She takes a new bulb up as if to carry on but her fingers freeze around it. Slowly she lifts her head.

Dew still glints on the lawn and the old evergreens along the boundary shiver and sigh in weak sunlight. The avocado is quite still. Olive turns quickly from it. There is no noise and nothing moves. The morning smells of cold and of winter.

Tilting her head she looks up. Above the trees and rooftops the sky is clear and pale. And there they are high above the garden.

It is the flock of silver birds. They fly bunched together and too high to be clearly seen but there is no mistaking the identity. What other flight can maintain such a speed? Which other birds are as nimble? They spin around and around in an ashen sky.

Dropping the trowel, Olive straightens up. She bends her head back to watch. The light is harsh. She shades her eyes with one hand.

Ducking and twisting, the birds fly directly overhead.

After a time a pain starts up in her neck. The posture is too difficult to hold. She sits on the damp lawn and leans back on her arms. Before long her elbows start to ache and she lies down on the grass.

Beneath her body the earth is immense and solid. Silence reaches up from its very depths. It carries a certain stillness. Only the birds dance in defiance of it.

Individuals dip and twist away from the group then rejoin it. No sooner has Olive's eye fixed upon a bird than it turns back into the flock and is lost. Their flight patterns alter but they maintain a clockwise direction. Their altitude and range are constant.

To the west and lower in the sky flat lilac clouds are stacking up.

There is a cry from somewhere behind. 'Olive, Olive?'

Jean is running down the garden path in a tight skirt. Her arms are out in front and a handbag swings wildly on one wrist.

'Ahh.' Olive rolls onto her stomach and rises stiffly on her elbows. She is on her knees now and climbing to her feet.

'What happened?' Jean screams.

'Nothing.'

'Did you collapse?'

'Ah no, I was just looking at something.'

'But it's all wet, how could you? You're all wet, look at your jacket! It's ruined! My God!'

Olive runs her hands down damp fabric at the back of her trousers. 'I was watching something.'

'Olive, I hope you don't mind me saying, I think you're being extremely irresponsible. I was ironing my blouse.

I have to be in town in less than an hour. I haven't even done my make-up. Eleven o'clock I'm meeting Jill, and I looked out the window and saw you lying on the lawn. I thought you'd been murdered or at least had a stroke. My hands are still shaking, look at them. Look at that. Trembling like a leaf.'

'Oh Jean, I'm so sorry. I wasn't thinking. But I was watching some birds and I think they're probably quite rare.'

Olive glances upwards and Jean catches her eye. They both look to the sky.

'Nothing,' Jean says.

'Nothing.'

'Hmm.'

'They were there for ages.' Olive exhales and something other than her lungs deflates inside.

The sky is blank and too pale. Her right eye twitches.

'You'd better change,' says Jean. 'Get into some dry clothes.'

'I will in a minute.'

'Are you all right?'

'Yes, of course I'm all right.'

'You shouldn't encourage birds, you know,' Jean says kindly. 'They foul the washing on the line. There's nothing worse than that, is there?'

'No, nothing. It's the worst thing in the world.'

'Let's go, or I'll be late.'

'Watching them isn't exactly the same thing as encouraging them.'

'I don't know about that. All those grey birds in your garden yesterday.'

'What grey birds?'

'They were everywhere.' Jean's forehead creases.

'What birds?'

'Pigeons.'

'Pigeons? Are you sure?'

'Yes, I am. I do know what pigeons look like. They had those sort of fan tails and nasty little heads.'

'I've never seen pigeons in the garden.'

'Someone around here must keep them. They're okay

in the country but the city is no place for birds.'

'How many were there?'

'Oh, I don't know. There was a whole lot. I rushed out and flapped a tablecloth at them and they flew away.'

'You did what?'

'I flapped a cloth at them.'

'Why?'

'What's the matter now?' Jean says. 'They were eating your grass seed.' She starts walking up the path towards the house.

Olive catches at her sleeve. 'What grass seed?'

'Mind my cuff. This material marks easily, it has acrylic in it. That's what I thought they were doing. They were picking away.'

'Oh dear!' Olive cries.

'What's wrong? I was doing you a favour. You don't want birds around. They've got revolting beady eyes and they foul the washing.'

'And they were pigeons, were they?'

'That's right. Look, I'm going to have to dash or I'll never make it to town.'

Jean hurries up the stairs. Clouds of steam sweep out through the back door.

'My goodness!' she says. 'In all the excitement I left the hot tap running!'

Olive stands at the top of the stairs. Leaning forward onto the rail she scans the sky. Long flat clouds are building up above the rooftops but the sun is unobstructed. It hangs in a pale lake.

If I could get higher I could see better, Olive thinks. The thought seems important.

'That's one thing wrong with the city,' she says stepping into the house.

'What is?'

'There's no horizon.'

Jean shakes a teatowel and steam swirls about the kitchen. 'What do you mean?'

'There's so many things crammed in. There's no proper horizon.'

The teatowel slaps down on the bench. 'Oh damn,' Jean

says. 'I do hope this steam hasn't ruined my hair. It's gone all flat, I can tell.'

Olive pulls the heavy door shut behind. 'I need to see a horizon.'

'You need to see a hairdresser. If you worried about real things, Olive, you'd be a lot happier. Of that there is no doubt at all.'

Turning away, Olive runs her fingers through her hair. She smiles to herself. I've seen the birds, she thinks. It's a Tuesday morning in the world and I've seen the silver birds. She holds the thought closely and is warmed by it.

Olive butters two squares of wholemeal bread and spreads them with chutney and slices of cheese. She takes the sandwiches to the table and positions her chair so the garden is clear through the window although the orchard and avocado are hidden from view.

She is alone in the house. Halfway through the food she loses interest. Pushing the plate back she stands up. She goes upstairs to the attic room.

A week has passed since the night of the storm. Her two paintings are vivid on the wall. She stands back to look at them.

Olive soon turns from the woman in the forest but the flying self-portrait fills her with delight. There is such freedom and beauty in the angle of her body floating high above the land and the dark hair sweeping out in a wave behind. The lemon skirts billow and puff.

Land and sea meet in a line of grey on blue. Olive visualises the horizon where it extends beyond the confines of the painting. It is so wide and curves away with the perfect symmetry of a globe.

I'm stuck to the ground, she thinks desperately. Her eyes feast on the picture. Stuck at ground level.

But in the attic room at least there is a feeling of elevation. In between the sloping roofs glimpses of the harbour glitter and when sparrows fly to the bamboo they pass at eye-level or lower. To look down on the back of a bird from above, she thinks as they skim by.

A heavy wooden ladder lies under the house. Olive waits for her eyes to adjust to the dim light then drags it out and wrestles it up against the back wall where the roof is flat and lower than the rest. She stands there panting.

The two ends of the ladder dig into the soil as Olive begins to climb. One hand grips while the other moves forward.

Near the top she looks down and her feet tingle with fear at the height. Calendula plants in the border look strangely squat from above. The flowers are circles of yellow and orange. The yellow are more plentiful but they are less than half the size.

Slowly Olive continues her ascent. Each time she is about to climb from the top of the ladder onto the roof, fear freezes her limbs. Finally she scrambles onto the iron. Taking a deep breath she stands up. Sweat runs in a line down her back.

The garden looks different from this height. The lawn stretches smooth as carpet and is shadowed in places by shrubs and trees. In the orchard the mass of bare branches and twigs blend to a soft lavender haze.

Six sparrows perch on the open orchard gate. One flies off and the others hop nervously before flinging themselves into the air.

A few steps behind her the roof slopes sharply upwards. Olive takes her shoes and socks off and leaning forward onto her hands begins to climb the slopes in bare feet.

The iron is warm and dry beneath her palms. Each sheet is corrugated. The feeling of it makes her sweat more. There is nothing to hold onto.

She dare not look back. Keep moving on. As it is, she is aware of a picture of herself lying broken on the path below. There would be nothing anyone could do. Pushing this thought away she concentrates on her hands and feet. She crawls slowly up the roof. Every muscle is taut.

At last she is sitting securely astride the ridge at the top. Taking a flattened cigarette from her pocket she places it in her mouth and strikes a match. Her fingers tremble and the flame flutters then holds.

The view is magnificent. Backyards stretch and join to

form wide green strips between the streets. Viridescent bands run down to the harbour. The water is a sheet of blue glass.

To the west, the undulating ridge of the Waitakere Ranges marks the boundary between land and sky.

'Oh!' cries Olive, and the sound bounces out happily into clean air. Drawing on the cigarette she swallows a cloud of smoke down then blows it out.

Looking at the dull blue of the harbour and the bright strips of green Olive thinks of her life. And she thinks about the birds. Mainly she thinks of the birds.

Her eye quivers and half shuts and the colours blend together. What don't I want to see? Don't want to see what's happening in my life. What is happening? Nothing.

Her eyes flicker and shut altogether and against the void of her eyelids the bright birds stream by. Flooding from the shadow of the house they fly into the cloudless light of day and in doing so change from black to silver.

Her eyes open and blink into focus. There is no sign of the birds in the sky but a number of seagulls pass swooping and wheeling on their way inland. Over the harbour they are white flecks but as they fly closer their bodies fill out.

Gliding over the roof their wings are fixed but their heads move from side to side and their eyes are ever-vigilant.

As the afternoon wears on, the distant hills deepen and the iron loses its heat. Olive stretches one leg then the other. She moves so she is no longer astride the ridge but sitting on it facing the street.

Several cars pass, then a blue taxi pulls up. The front passenger door opens and Jean spills out. Her arms bulge with bags and parcels. Putting a box down on the footpath she returns to pay the driver through the window. The car slides away.

'Jean, Jean!' Olive calls. 'Up here!'

Jean looks over her shoulder and down the street. She juggles her parcels and pushes the front gate with the toe of her shoe.

'On the roof! I'm on the roof!'

Jean stands just inside the gate. The camellia brushes her arm on one side. She looks around in all directions except up.

'Raise your vision!' Olive bellows and her voice cracks.

I must look so silly, she thinks, and then she is laughing. A middle-aged woman on the roof. A housewife. In ill-fitting tartan pants and cold bare feet and deep half moons etched beneath my eyes where once the flesh was plump. Ah, where once the flesh was plump.

Olive touches her face. She can feel the sharp cheekbone.

Jean has moved from sight. The front door slams.

Sparrows line up along the powerlines in the street below. They form small groups and clumps. Olive tries to count them but the birds move and her eyelids flutter. What don't I want to see?

Jim arrives home next. The car slows in the street and swings crunching gravel into the driveway.

After a moment he appears at the gate. He plucks a newspaper from the letterbox.

'Hello, hello!' Olive cries.

He glares about.

'Up here on the roof!'

'Olive!' he calls.

'I'm on the roof!'

His lips move but the words are too faint to carry.

'You're stuck to the ground!' she roars.

He disappears into the house.

To imagine Jim and Jean moving in the house below while I perch on the roof above, Olive thinks. It is a different dimension. She smiles and shifts her weight.

A small boat cuts across the harbour. The water is dark now and choppy. When did the change occur?

The sail is a white triangle bobbing and starting. At times the hull seems almost submerged. The distance creates such a distortion.

From the lounge chimney lower on the gable a meagre line of smoke appears. It drifts up sleepily then suddenly thickens and blows out over the roof. It smells of burning blue gum.

Olive begins inching down the roof. She moves on her bottom with her hands flat against the iron on either side. She walks over the flat section and lowers herself onto the ladder. Her joints are stiff and cold.

Jean is slicing button mushrooms at the kitchen table. A stiff white apron covers her dress and her hair is swept back into a wave.

A pile of tomatoes stands at the centre of the table. The larger ones are at the bottom. There is a purple eggplant and a large green avocado alongside.

Tilting the chopping board, Jean slides the knife blade across and pink and white slivers of mushroom fall into a bowl. 'There you are,' she says.

'Hello.' Taking the avocado Olive cups it in her hand as if to test the weight. She strokes it with her thumb, feeling both the cold in her fingers and the bald texture of the fruit.

'Where have you been?' Jean asks.

Olive looks up to the ceiling. 'I don't know if our avocado is this sort or the other sort.'

'What avocado?'

'The tree.'

'What other sort?'

'Some are small and dark, almost black. And they're very bumpy.'

'I prefer these ones.'

'I wonder if I'll ever know what sort ours is,' Olive says. 'I don't think I will.'

'I didn't know you had one.'

'It's down the back. It's never fruited and I don't think it will now.'

'You have no shoes on, Olive.'

'They're at the back door.'

'Your feet are purple.'

'Yes.'

Jean tightens her lips. Fine lines run up from her lipstick.

'Have you had a good day?' Olive asks.

Jean takes the eggplant in one hand and the chopping knife in the other. She pushes the blade through, sending the two halves falling away from each other. The inside is white and spongy.

'I've been shopping.'

'Did you buy these vegetables?'

'I did. I thought I'd cook tonight. You don't mind, do you?'

'No, of course not. But you're away from home you shouldn't bother.'

'It's no bother,' Jean snaps.

'No, no, let me. Really, I'd feel happier.'

Jean's movements are slow and deliberate. She places the knife on the board and straightens her apron. 'Look,' she says. 'I know what it's like when you don't feel one hundred percent.'

Olive is confused. She puts the avocado down and rubs her hands together. The fruit rolls over twice on the table and comes to rest. She folds her arms and rubs her feet one on top of the other.

'What do you mean?'

'You used to be a very good cook, Olive.'

'Oh.'

'Don't worry. You'll get back into it when you're feeling better.'

'But I'm fine. Cooking is no problem.'

'That fish pie you cooked last night was the worst fish pie I have ever had,' Jean says. 'It was dreadful.'

Olive's hand flies to her mouth. 'Was it?'

'It was appalling and your lemon pudding didn't rise at all.'

'I know, but it wasn't me it was the eggs. They were odd eggs. The whites wouldn't whip.'

'You just add a little salt for that.'

'But I did.'

'After working all day Jim deserves at the very least to come home to a decent meal. Don't be upset. I'm only telling you because I care. You know that. It doesn't matter. I'll cook for a few days and you can have a rest, then you'll feel more like it.'

'I thought the fish pie was quite nice.'

'Ugh. I don't believe you. It tasted like glue.'

'I see.' Olive rushes from the room.

Twilight sends shadows through the house. The fire is the single source of illumination in the lounge. Jim stands at the mantelpiece. He pours sherry from a crystal decanter into a small glass.

'What's wrong?' he asks. 'Come over here so I can see you.'

'Hello.'

'Your face is flushed,' he says, peering at her. 'What's wrong? Where have you been?'

'Jean told me my fish pie tasted like glue.'

'What fish pie?'

'The one we had for dinner last night.'

He is looking at the floor now. 'What on earth are you doing in bare feet?'

'My shoes are at the back door. Was it that bad?'

'Come closer to the fire. You'll get chilblains on a night like this.'

'The pie?'

'It was fairly horrible.'

'You didn't say so at the time.'

'No, I just left it on my plate.'

'Was it really bad?'

'If you really want to know it was absolutely appalling.' Anger breaks into his voice.

'I didn't realise.'

'Well, now you know.'

'But there's half of it left. What am I going to do with it?'

'Plaster the path.'

'Jean's cooking tonight.'

'I know she is.' Jim sips the amber liquid and rolls it on his tongue.

'She bought an avocado.'

'Mm.'

'Did you have a good day?'

'Yes, we had a seminar today.'

'A seminar?'

'Yes, very interesting. Big lunch.'

'We live in different worlds, you and I,' Olive says.

Jim brushes a speck from his jacket and looks at her. He is frowning. 'You're letting yourself slip.'

'My shoes are at the door.'

'A bit of make-up would help. And if you did something with your hair.'

'I've had a good day today,' Olive says. 'I've been very happy today.'

'What did you do?'

'I took the ladder out and climbed up onto the roof and I looked at the view.'

'Bloody Christ,' Jim mutters. 'Here we go.'

'The seagulls were flying inland all afternoon. That usually means a storm, I know, although it doesn't seem the weather for one.'

'Shall I pour you a sherry?'

'Yes please.'

'And what did you really do today?'

'I went into town and shopped for shoes. I bought some taupe shoes to match my handbag.'

Jim replaces the decanter. He passes a full glass of sherry. Relief eases the movement of his arm. 'Good,' he says. 'Cheers.'

'Cheers.'

With sudden violence the two glasses crash together. Olive holds hers to the fire and examines it for a fracture. The glass is intact. Little diamonds of light flare and fade from the pattern cut around the rim as she turns it and the sherry tilts from side to side. A drop runs down the side and falls to the floor.

Jim holds his glass lightly by the stem. His hands are impeccably groomed.

Olive takes a drink to Jean.

The avocado is in two halves now. Where the stone has been removed from the middle of each piece the flesh is indented. It runs from green at the outside into cream but in the shadow of the hollow the colour deepens to yellow.

'Can I have the stone?' Olive asks.

'What stone?'

'The avocado stone. I'd like to germinate it.'
'What for?'
'I don't know.'
'I threw it out.'
Olive lifts the lid of the rubbish container. The bag is filled almost to the top with boxes and jars and vegetables.
Jean clears her throat. 'I had a little clean-out in your cupboards. You keep all this old food.'
'This isn't old. Jean, all this food!' Olive takes a potato and puts it on the bench.
'They're sprouting. You've got a whole cupboard full of sprouting potatoes.'
'But there's nothing wrong with these potatoes.'
'They're old. I bought some fresh ones.'
'There's a whole box of cornflakes!'
'They're stale.'
'They are not. They're fine. You can't throw all this food out.'
'You can't eat it.'
'I don't put vegetables in the rubbish,' Olive says. 'I put them in the compost.'
'It's not hygienic.'
'What's not?'
'You put your scraps in that bucket and it smells.'
'But I empty it into the compost. I need it for the garden. It's a waste to throw vegetables in the rubbish.'
'I've been shopping, Olive. Everything's replaced.'
'But it's such a waste! I made this chutney.'
'You made it a year ago. Last time I was here.'
'Chutney keeps for ages.'
'Everything's replaced and tidied up.'
Olive gropes amongst the food in the rubbish bag and her fingers feel the stone hard and slippery before she sees it.
'The feeling of it makes you think of a new-born baby.'
'Do you have any more pepper? The pepper mill is empty.'
'Oh!' says Olive. The stone has been cut into deeply all the way around. The soft wood inside shows as a pale slash.

'I'm looking for the pepper.'

'It won't grow,' she says sadly. The stone falls back into the rubbish.

Jean takes boxes of spices from the cupboard and piles them on the bench. A yellow stream of turmeric spills out.

'I'm sorry,' Olive says. 'I think I forgot to get pepper.'

Jean sighs with annoyance. 'Pepper steak,' she says. 'Without the pepper.'

'I'll get some tomorrow.'

'What's wrong with your eye?'

'Nothing.'

'It's twitching. I do wish you'd go to the doctor.'

Olive lies on her side in bed. Jim's knees are in the small of her back. She leans against him to no effect. He has been asleep for some time.

Shutting her eyes, she strains for a picture of the birds. They are vague at first then vivid in her mind. Dark birds roll and coil with beauty and agility. The May sky is bleached and clear of cloud.

Warm beneath the weight of winter blankets Olive clings to this image.

It fades and at the same moment sleep comes. It is a blank.

After a time the image returns in the form of a dream. The birds are in the air again.

Olive watches them. The way they spin and turn. She glances away for a moment and that time is all it takes for them to disappear. The sky is quite empty.

It is a harsh landscape. Bare hills rise and plunge steeply. Great slabs of land pile together and fall away into the valleys between. The light is pale for twilight or dawn.

Olive stands on a narrow path of clay cut high along the side of a hill. The land is barren but pine trees grow along the way. Wind in the high branches makes a sound like the sea.

Olive discovers that the coat she is wearing is the same brown one she had worn as a child of ten. In some places the fabric has worn thin and the brown has weakened to grey. There is a hood attached and a band of bumpy black material. The buttons are black to match.

Her fingers skim down the front. One button is missing.

The coat fits perfectly. Olive doesn't feel any smaller, but neither does the garment seem larger.

There is no surprise at finding it fitting so well. She examines it with a mixture of pleasure and grief.

She steadies herself on the clay path. Her feet are set apart for the balance.

Something moves along her arm, making a bulge in the sleeve of her coat. She watches the progress and also feels it. The shape is at her wrist now and pushing through. It shoots out from her cuff and into the air. A silver bird flies away.

She lifts the other arm and a bird appears from that sleeve also.

One by one they fly from her sleeves as if it is a circus act. Each new bird joins the others, circling high above the hill. They spin in a clockwise direction.

The movement of the birds in her sleeves is sensuous, but at her wrists where the cuffs are tighter they flutter and rip at her skin with needle claws. Sharp pain stabs at her wrists.

The last bird is larger and the cuffs have tightened. It struggles to be free and its feet lash backwards and forwards, lacerating the soft skin along the underside of her arm.

'I'll get blood on my coat.' Startled by the statement she awakens.

The bedside clock ticks quietly in the dark. Luminous hands show the time at twenty past three.

Olive rises onto her elbows. The blind is up and an oblong of moonlight glows at the foot of the bed. Jim's legs are a shadowy bump in the middle of it. Facing the wall he sleeps soundly.

Olive turns from one side to the other. Her wrists continue to sting and her breath is quick and shallow as if here in the bedroom she still breathes the thin air of high hill country.

'A dream, a dream,' she whispers, but the discomfort

is intense.

Pulling the blankets back she gets up and goes out to the kitchen. Switching the light on she leans back on the bench. I'll make a drink. She puts milk to warm on the stove and measures Milo and sugar into a cup.

While adding the sugar Olive sees the blood. At one moment she is watching white crystals of sugar flowing from the spoon and in the next moment her vision is filled with scarlet streaks of blood. Red lines run along her wrists and disappear beneath the sleeves of her nightdress.

Spraying out sugar, the spoon flies to the floor. Olive slumps back into a chair. Her arms are on her lap and she stares straight ahead. I am cut, she thinks, and I bleed. She lifts her arms onto the table and examines them.

The blood has come from superficial cuts criss-crossed through her flesh. In places it is dry and caked but the cuts are fresh clean lines. At one spot on her right wrist minute beads of blood still swell.

Milk rises in the pot on the oven behind and runs hissing onto the element. Olive jumps up and snatches it away. The kitchen fills with the smell of burning. She pours the remaining hot milk into a cup and returns to the table.

The discomfort eases. Sipping the hot drink Olive looks at the cuts without feeling. That they should be there in the middle of the night doesn't seem unnatural. I'm cut and I bleed. Ahh, she thinks.

After drinking the milk Olive returns to bed. Both arms hug tight around her chest. She slips back easily into sleep.

Shortly before dawn there is another dream but the birds don't reappear and she doesn't think to look for them.

Olive stands looking out across a wide body of water. Near the shore it is calm and black. A massive storm rages far out at sea. Along the horizon the water is white and the sky is alternately dark and bright with sheets of neon lightning.

Olive has to swim across the water. She has been told this although there is no one there to have told her. She knows it to be true.

Her destination is somewhere on the other side and there is no vessel.

She is far too fearful to enter the water, but in the next moment she finds herself swimming well out from land. It is cold and deep and the strange storm rages all around. There is this feeling of water on her body and the awareness of depth below.

She is afraid. There is no option but to swim. She presses on and on. The panic keeps her company.

Olive is still moving through dark water when she awakens. Surprised, she pushes one hand through the sheets.

In the bamboo outside sparrows sing for a new day. Watery bands of light flicker on the bedroom walls.

Jim stirs alongside. Opening his eyes he stretches one arm above his head. 'Mm,' he says.

Hold me, Olive thinks. Reach out for me now.

He squints at the window then sits up. 'You've slept late.'

Deep black water. Love me or I'll drown. It is a child's voice. 'Ahh,' she cries.

'Time to get up,' he says.

She remembers the cuts on her wrists. With her arms tucked into her armpits Olive wriggles from the bed. She hurries past and to the bathroom.

Locking the door she stands leaning against it. She gently eases her sleeves back and her breath pulls in. There are no cuts.

Dried blood cakes the fabric of her cuffs and the blackbird's bloodstain is rich and ominous on her right hand but the skin stretching up from it and onto her wrists is pink and unmarked.

'Oh Jesus,' Olive whispers in her throat.

Nothing makes sense. I can't go on.

'Hold me, hold me,' she says to the bathroom door.

The bathroom door is wood. It makes no response.

There are no traces of blood in the kitchen but the saucepan stands where she left it on the bench. The sides are still sticky where milk surged down and her cup is on the table. The bottom is brown with traces of Milo.

The floor is gritty with sugar. Near the wall, ants swarm about. They carry the sugar off rather than eat it. Each ant carries a grain and they march in single file.

Olive steps around them. She plugs the toaster in and slices tomatoes into a pan. Standing back, she rubs her eyes and runs her fingers through her hair.

Opening the fridge door she looks inside. The remaining fish pie is in a dish near the bottom. Taking it out she lifts it to her nose. There is no smell at all.

While the breakfast is cooking she goes out through the back door and down into the garden. She places the fish pie still in its dish on the lawn near the orchard gate.

'A cat will get it,' she says, turning back towards the house.

Jim leaves for work and Jean is not yet up.

Olive returns to bed. Pulling the bedding back she pushes her legs in. Any warmth from her body or from Jim's has cooled. A scarlet mark catches her eye.

On the upper sheet on her side there are a number of bloodstains. Some of them overlap as if someone has taken a fine red pen and drawn thin lines and dots upon the sheet, but the colour is that of blood rather than ink.

Olive nestles down into the bed and pulls the covers up tight around her shoulders. Unaccustomed feelings of tenderness wash over her. It is a preciousness appropriate to having been wounded. She nurses her injuries.

That they aren't real is of little consequence.

The strips of light on the walls are higher now and bold and yellow. Olive watches them quiver.

CHAPTER EIGHT

DOROTHY'S DOOR IS unlocked and Olive lets herself in. 'Hello, hello, it's only me,' she calls.

The old house is cold and silent. It smells musty as if deserted. Weak sunlight filters through a pane of amber glass above the door at the end of the hall.

Olive tiptoes in that direction. She puts the plant she is carrying down on the floor and taps on the bedroom door. There is no reply and she taps again. Pushing the door open, she enters the room.

Dorothy sits half turned away in the bed. She is lost in the gloom. Alarmed, she spins around and plump fingers slap over her mouth.

'Oh Olive!' she cries. Her hand drops and something rolls in her mouth then she swallows and smiles. Brown specks stick to her teeth in the front.

'I'm so glad to see you. But you caught me in the act.' She takes a lumpy piece of fruit-cake from beneath the covers.

'Are you all right?' Olive asks. 'The house was so quiet. It felt like there was nobody here.'

'Here I am. The days just come and go.'

'Are you well?'

'No, not really, but I'm okay, if you know what I mean.'

Dorothy uncovers a larger slab of cake. The cut side is yellow and studded with currants and glistening red cherries. She brushes it down with a paper serviette. Crumbs fall into the bed.

'Would you make a cup of tea? Let's have a nice cup of tea.'

Olive goes out to the kitchen. She fills the hot-water

jug and plugs it in. The bench is strewn with dirty dishes and sodden tea-leaves line the bottom of the sink.

A frying-pan of fat congeals on the stove. Three and a half swollen sausages are embedded in it and neat indentations indicate where another two have been.

The half-sausage has been bitten rather than cut. Teeth marks show clearly on it.

Olive looks at the half-eaten sausage and the curving line of marks. She looks at the thick layer of fat and feels like crying.

There is a brown-paper bag on the table. Reaching into it she takes two packets of biscuits out and a chocolate cake wrapped in cellophane. She puts the cake in the fridge. The shelves are full of paper bags and foil wrappers. Two lettuces wilt at the bottom.

There is no milk for the tea. She pours it black and takes two steaming cups into the bedroom on a tray.

'I've been thinking about food,' she says.

'Yes I do a lot of that.'

'What I'm wondering is . . .'

'Is what?'

'Well, do you think if you cook without love your food tastes bad? Or even goes rotten? You know, before it should. Even if the ingredients are right and you follow the recipe and everything? And try really hard?'

'I've never thought of it like that. I don't bake these days. I just get Frank to buy things from the supermarket. They make these lovely muffins on Thursdays. Carrot-and-bran or banana. The banana ones are moist but they have less sultanas, I find.'

'I can't cook any more.'

'You're a good cook, Olive. Everyone knows that.'

'I was, but I can't do it any more. Recipes just don't work. Even the old ones.'

'They will again.'

'I sort of think they won't if I don't cook with love. I don't seem to have it to put into food. Or the family. I can't really explain what I mean.'

Dorothy's mouth slides about on her face as if she doesn't know what to make it say. She smiles sadly and bites into a piece of cake.

The chrysanthemums Olive brought last time are still in their vase beside the bed. The flowers are finished but still intact. The petals are dry and brown and curled around and the vase is empty of water.

'I bought you a plant,' says Olive. She gets it from the hall.

It is a cyclamen in a pot. Eight cerise flowers stand up on stalks above firm leaves and fat buds bend their heads on shorter stems.

'Oh,' says Dorothy. 'It's so beautiful.'

Olive moves the vase of dead flowers and runs her hand across the table-top. It leaves a slash through the dust. She puts the plant down.

'So there are things out there still growing?'

'It's winter now.'

'But some things still grow?'

'Yes, some things grow in the cold.'

'It might be from a glasshouse.'

'I don't know.'

They both look at the plant. Pink and green are bright together. In this room it is the only thing of solid colour. It takes on a.tropical air.

'I should be up,' says Dorothy. 'But I can't be bothered.'

'There's no rush. Take it easy.'

'What have you been doing?'

Olive picks at her thumb-nail. The skin is rough at the edge. 'I don't know. Nothing much springs to mind.'

'Have you been out?'

'No, not really. Jim's sister is still staying.'

'How is her boy?'

'She hasn't even been to see him yet. She's been with us for weeks now but there's always a reason for not going. For a whole week she couldn't go because it rained and her high heels would get stuck in the lawn at the hospital.'

'Do those sorts of hospitals have lawns?'

'I shouldn't think so.'

'You're not enjoying her company?'

'No, not really. She leaves the hot taps running. I can't

bear to see all that hot water running down the sink.'

Dorothy's round face creases into a smile. Her eyes swing back to the plant.

'We're both going to be grandmothers,' Olive says. 'Michael and his wife are expecting a baby.'

'Olive, how lovely.'

'I've hardly given it a thought. I've always looked forward to grandchildren but I don't feel any great interest. Not yet anyway. I'm sure I should.'

'You're not knitting little white bonnets?'

'No.'

'No lemon booties?'

'Not even one. Are you?'

'No,' Dorothy says, hacking at the cake. 'Would you like another slice?'

'I don't think I will, thank you.'

A cherry falls from the piece of cake. It rolls on the bedspread and onto the floor.

Olive retrieves it and puts it on the table. The sticky surface is coated with thick grey dust.

Olive leaves Dorothy's house by the same door through which she entered. She stops at the bottom of the stairs.

The backyard dips down in the centre and is surrounded on all sides by elevated properties. In the middle of the garden a great jacaranda tree reaches up. Its barren branches spread as if to shut out the houses looking down from the slopes all around.

There is a sound like running water. Stepping down into the garden Olive turns her head to listen. Water trickles from a drain at the back of the house and runs across the path, making a dark stain on the concrete. Thick emerald grass marks its course through the lawn until it ends in a swampy area below the base of the jacaranda. Weeds spring up in the stagnant damp.

The tree is winter bare and grey with moss. Its nakedness somehow accentuates the low-lying aspect of the land.

Olive prods the swampy soil with her foot. There is nowhere else for the water to drain to. Everything else is higher.

Moving back towards the jacaranda, she reaches out behind until her hands are touching the trunk. She feels the bark and it is smooth and dry and warmer than the chill of the day.

In the hollow between two hills Olive struggles for breath. Drowning, she thinks, and her mouth is open. She draws the new air in.

She hurries over the lawn to the path. It follows the side of the house back towards the street.

Outside Dorothy's room Olive stops and looks up. The window is blank with heavy curtains. Little light can reach in. No sound passes through.

Leaning against the wall beneath the window sill she lights a cigarette. Blue smoke drifts up and glances off the glass.

Olive closes her eyes until she can see her friend inside the stale room. Her big belly and breasts heave from one side to the other as she moves in the bed.

Sitting down on the path, Olive sucks the cigarette. Flax bushes grow in a border on the other side and they are backed by the weatherboard wall of the house next door. Paint flakes off in long shards. The exposed wood is pale below.

She looks up at the windows. One of them is open. No one stands there looking down.

A broad band of sky shows between the roofs. Even as she watches, the colour deepens. Pewter clouds roll across.

When the first cigarette has finished Olive lights another from the butt. She smokes this one halfway through, then stubs it out on the path. She rises and returns to the back door of the house. It opens quietly.

The bedroom door is ajar as she left it. Small sounds come from the room but when Dorothy turns the white moon of her face it is dry.

'Olive,' she says. 'Did you forget something?'

'I was going to tell you something.'

'And you came back?'

'Yes.'

'I hope you hadn't gone far.'

Olive shakes her head.

Dorothy pulls herself upright and pushes at the pillows until she is comfortable. 'What is it?'

'You see,' Olive says awkwardly. 'One day I climbed onto the roof.'

'The roof?'

'The roof of our house.'

'I'm with you.'

'And.'

'Yes?' Dorothy says.

'I sat on the roof at the top. The very top.'

'Help, I'd be far too scared.'

'Yes.'

'To sit on the roof.'

'Yes.'

'It's a long way up.'

'Yes it is,' says Olive.

'Is that what you came back to tell me?'

'Ah, yes.'

'Oh.'

'You can see a long way from up there. That's the point.'

'I bet you can, too.'

'You can see the Waitakeres from one end to the other.'

'You'd see right over the harbour, I suppose.'

'You can,' says Olive. 'I can't see anything from the ground.'

'Nor can I. I never wanted to buy in this hollow but there you are.'

'But I mean I can't see anything from the ground. Really. I can't see where I'm going.'

'No.'

'Dorothy, I can't even see what I want.'

'No.'

'And — ah — you can see such a lot from up there. You really can.'

'Tell you what, then,' Dorothy says. 'Next time you're going up onto the roof give me a call and I'll catch a taxi over.'

'We'll sit up there together.'

'I'll wear my nighty.'

'Wear that big cream one you had on last time I was here.'

'The big cream one with lace?'

'Yes. We might see something we like the look of from up there.'

'Yes. We can look out over the roof and your nighty can blow in the breeze. Crack like a sail.'

They laugh, but Olive's face is quick to twist. Tears fall down her cheeks then they are both crying.

Hold me, Olive thinks. Love me or I'll drown. Dorothy's arms reach out. Her great breasts are pillows.

They cry and cry.

In time a silence descends.

'I have to go,' Olive says. 'I think it's going to rain.'

Halfway home the rain starts. The first heavy drops splash onto the path around her feet as Olive walks down the slope of Albert Park. Almost instantly, the dark spots run together and the whole path is glistening and wet. It is a deluge. The rising scent is a mixture of asphalt and rain.

Olive dashes for the cover of a Moreton Bay fig. Twisting roots thick as boughs radiate out in ridges and hollows from the base of the trunk. The folds resemble flesh in some way. It is the smoothness of them. Aerial roots reach down from the branches above.

A narrow thread of water snakes down the grey trunk, curving on its contours to the ground. Diagonal lines of rain batter their rhythm on the cover of leaves. Beneath the tree it is dry.

Olive moves back between the protruding roots. Pulling her coat tightly against the cold she looks out across the park.

A maple stands alone on the grass. The tree rains leaves. The force of the downpour strips it of the last of its autumn foliage and the brown leaves swirl in a gentle descending skirt.

A man and two women run downhill along the path. The circles of their umbrellas bump and pull away. One of the women bounds ahead and the other two slow to a walk. Laughter soars up the slope. It could be the man's laughter or it might be one of the women. The sound causes Olive to feel alone. I am alone, she thinks.

Rain drums on the canopy above and whirs in the lower foliage and deeper and lower still is the hum of the city below. Car horns sound in the distance.

Sheets of water carrying twigs and leaves fan out over bare ground beneath tall trees on the hillside.

Olive leans back against the trunk and lights a cigarette. Breathing the smoke out, she studies the mass of branches and leaves above and the specks of sky where it shows rich and grey. In some places the rain cloud appears deep enough to be blue.

Her eye falls upon a cluster of aerial roots. They reach down from a branch overhead. Some are thick and wooden and others splay into fine hair at the ends. There is something about the way they hang.

That's my sorrow, Olive thinks. The longer she looks at the roots the stronger the thought becomes. A relationship between the shapes they make and her sadness increases until the two are inseparable.

My sorrow hangs from the trees. The thought is not without comfort. Although the roots are blind and reaching, the forms they make are pleasing. They possess a sort of beauty. A sad beauty. Olive is attracted to it. Perhaps I choose that she thinks, but she is pushing the thought away. Ahh.

The deluge eases. Olive stands there looking out.

Everything flows downwards. The rain and the sheets of surface water where they seek lower ground. An occasional leaf still falls from the maple. And in the flowerbed, plants are bent, some of them parallel to the ground.

All movement is downwards. Everything is falling. It seems too much.

The rain stops and people appear on the paths again. They stride down the hill or walk gingerly for fear of slipping. Two elderly women go past hand in hand.

Defiantly, Olive takes an uphill route but the direction is wrong and when she reaches the upper boundary of the park there is little choice but to turn and retrace her steps.

Passing the Moreton Bay fig she pauses. The outermost branches quiver and shed crystal drops of water. They spot her coat and fall cold onto her scalp. A thin trickle of water runs down her neck. She savours the sensation.

The aerial roots hang still in mid-air.

'Ahh,' Olive says. 'My sorrow hangs from the trees.'

Each step away takes her further down the hill.

Olive has a pen and paper at the breakfast table. In between sips of coffee she writes a list. She is planning the evening meal.

'Goodbye,' Jim calls from the door.

'Goodbye.'

'I'll cook tonight,' she says when Jean appears from her room.

'Are you sure?'

'Yes, I've planned it. The twins are coming.'

'If you're sure. I'm quite happy to,' Jean says. The bathroom door clicks shut behind her.

'I'm going to make a pavlova,' Olive calls.

A rush of water from the bathroom drowns her words. The shower curtain zips across.

Olive gets her shopping bag from the hall cupboard. Leaving the house, she takes the uphill route, stopping at the dairy on the way.

'Have you any free-range eggs?' she says.

The shopkeeper is hanging bags of bright pink sweets on hooks above the counter. He takes them from a white box.

'Nup,' he says. 'Not a one.'

'Ah. Will you be getting any?'

'I don't know. I'll see what I can do. How are the twins?'

'The twins? They're fine. They're always fine.'

'You're lucky. Indeed you are lucky to have daughters like those two.'

'I have another daughter, Annette.'

'We don't see her around.'

'If I can't get free-range at the shops I'll call in on the way back and get carton eggs.'

'You do that.'

A bag of sweets falls and bursts on the floor near Olive's feet. Sweets shoot out in all directions. They bounce and roll, bright as plastic.

The shopkeeper laughs and pulls his moustache. 'They keep doing that,' he says.

Olive steps outside and looks around. The girl with the cigarettes is there. She is picking something up from the footpath.

Her blouse is purple satin and she wears high silver shoes. Her legs are bare and mottled with cold. Straightening her back she takes one uncertain step forward. She holds a packet of cigarettes. A partly smoked one protrudes between her fingers.

As Olive walks past, the girl snaps her hand shut around the hard pink spot of a sweet. Even in the strange shoes she barely reaches Olive's shoulder. From the corner of her eye Olive sees the movement of the girl's arm and when she glances back the sweet is a bulge in her cheek.

The girl's lips are full and curved. She wears no make-up and her hair is unkempt. She is too small. And cold. Her legs are cold.

Olive crosses the street. Reaching the other side she takes her purse from her bag and rushes back to the dairy. As she passes the girl she lets the purse drop from her hand as if by accident and hurries into the shop.

Bent from the waist, the shopkeeper sweeps sweets into a dustpan.

'Hello.'

He looks up and his face is red. 'Carton eggs after all?' he says, putting the broom aside.

'Ah yes . . . ah . . . no.' Olive takes a bottle of tomato sauce from a shelf then puts it back.

Moving further down she takes a can of fish and examines the label. The paper is blue and letters in black type run together. 'No added salt' is printed in white.

'I'll just look for a bit.'

'Feel free.' He steps through to the back of the shop.

Olive holds the flat top of the can to her cheek where the skin burns and it feels like ice.

The man returns with a can in his hand. 'Tuna,' he

says. 'Very good fish, tuna.'

'Yes, it is nice.'

'Good price, too.'

'I'll take one.' Olive rattles through her bag. 'I must have left my purse at home,' she says.

'Don't worry. Pay me later.'

Olive drops the fish into her bag and steps out through the door. Both the girl and the purse have vanished.

'You're back quickly,' Jean says, looking up.

Olive puts her bag on the table. 'I lost my purse.'

'Olive, you're hopeless.'

'But I did get some fish.'

'Tuna, how horrible. It's horrible fish.'

'I got it for the cat.'

'You don't have a cat.'

'No, but in case we get one.'

Jean squeezes lemon-coloured cream from a bottle onto her hands then rubs them together. She looks at Olive suspiciously.

'What is it?'

'You're not thinking of making another fish pie, are you?'

'No, I got it for the cat.'

Olive waits outside the bank until it opens. She withdraws a replacement amount of housekeeping money.

The supermarket is out of eggs. The wire racks where they are usually stacked are empty. She selects kumara and a large cauliflower and pays at the checkout.

Once outside she sets off walking for the next block of shops.

'Eggs?' the woman behind the counter says. 'Of course. We always have them.'

But a few minutes later she returns to make her apology. 'I'm sorry,' she says. 'We must have sold out.'

Clouds scud across the sky and the wind is cold but there are plenty of people about. Children call on the footpath and a puppy barks. Two men run past in shorts.

A petrol tanker pulls over and stops. Exhaust fumes combine with the smell of hot bread from the bakery.

The next shop is also eggless. 'We're right out,' the

woman explains.

'I'll call back another time.' Olive turns to leave but the woman continues.

'My brother-in-law's got a poultry farm,' she says. 'Up north, you know. He's got six thousand chooks and he got seven eggs last week. We were talking to him on the phone. It's hilarious. I laughed my head off until I was nearly sick.'

'Ah,' says Olive. 'Still, it's winter. You can't expect them to lay so well in winter.'

'But they use batteries.'

'Batteries, do they?'

'Ha ha. Six thousand chooks and seven eggs. I nearly died.'

'You're back again.' Jean pats her hair.

'The twins want pavlova but I couldn't get eggs.'

'Pavlova. That would be nice.'

'But there are no eggs.'

'Of course there are.'

'I've been everywhere. I'll have to go back to the dairy.'

'You'll get there,' Jean says. 'In the end.'

The shopkeeper grins. He puts both hands on the counter. 'Eggs,' he says. 'Sorry.'

'I thought you had carton eggs this morning.'

'I did. But they've all gone. I've had a run on eggs.'

'Ah, I see.'

'There's powdered egg, but.'

'I want them for pavlova.'

'Perhaps not, then.'

As Olive steps out through the shop doorway another bag of sweets falls behind her back. Pink lollies are everywhere around her feet and spilling out onto the footpath.

She moves away. Fatigue slows her limbs. Walking downhill is not so difficult. She fumbles with her key at the door.

Jean has gone out. Her perfume persists but the house is still. Olive checks every room to be sure.

She climbs the stairs to the attic and sits down on the

floor near the window. The bird marks dance ever-frozen in their poses on the sill.

Lying down she stretches out. Sleep comes and she submits.

Eggs jumble through her mind. They start off as plain brown eggs then elongate and open and change.

Olive is putting a brown-paper bag of shopping into the back seat of the car. She takes a seat beside Jim. There are no eggs now, but something moves and a flounder leaps from the bag onto the floor of the car.

Olive stretches around and takes it in her hands. Its spine arches and curves.

'It's still alive,' she says.

Jim's attitude is disapproving. 'It's a cup,' he says. 'Anyone could see that.'

'A cup?'

He pours fruit juice onto the fish. In some way it does seem to behave as a cup, but it is still a fish. Grey eyes roll and bulge.

Olive is aware of the feeling of scales on her hands. They are wet and slippery.

Some people stroll past the car and Jim calls out a greeting. Turning back, they look in through the windows. They are looking at the fish.

'It's very old china,' a woman says. 'You can tell by the handle and the rim is smooth.'

'Yes, and these vertical lines,' says Jim.

Olive gets out of the car and walks away over a flat area of grass. She can see her hand half curled but it really is her hand. She looks at the small lines in the arch between her thumb and forefinger. Her head lifts slowly to the light of the attic room.

Three hours have passed. Leaping to her feet she rushes down the stairs. Her legs are unsteady.

None of the shops have restocked with eggs. Olive repeats the morning's route then turns off into another street. She pounds the footpaths into a neighbouring area but her search is unrewarded.

'Is there a shortage of eggs?' she asks a shop assistant.

'No,' the girl replies. 'We've just run out.'
'But I can't get them anywhere.'
The girl smiles apologetically. 'Sorry,' she says.
Olive takes a packet of ice cream from the freezer and puts it on the counter. 'Have you any apples?' she asks.
'Over there.'
The fruit are shiny and red. She chooses a number of them.
Outside on the footpath she puts the things into her bag. Traffic has increased on the roads. People are driving home from work. The day has just gone.
There are no eggs and I have nothing done. The sense of urgency increases. Olive hurries home. The distance is considerable.
She is at the back door at last and turning her key in the lock.
She begins preparations for the meal immediately. Slapping the rimu board down she chops celery and carrots.
Jean and the twins come into the kitchen. 'Hello,' Heather says. 'We didn't know you were here.'
'I've just come in from the shops.'
'The shops?' Jean says. 'You're cooking dinner in your coat.'
'Ah yes.' Olive slips the garment off and throws it over a chair.
'You're a bit flushed,' Ruth says.
'I've been rushing.'
'How's that pavlova?'
'I couldn't buy eggs.'
'No eggs?' they shout. Heather lifts saucepan lids and Ruth opens the oven door.
'Where's all the food?'
'I'm running a bit late.'
'Does this mean no pavlova?'
'I'm afraid it does.'
'Piss poor,' says Ruth.
'Well, it better be good, whatever it is.' Heather prods Olive in the side. 'How's your skinny little ribs?'
'The thinner I get,' Olive says, 'the bigger you two grow. I've noticed that.'

'We're building our muscles.'
'For the summer look.'
'What look is that?'
'The strong look,' Ruth says. Her white teeth flash.
They bound from the room. Jean stays for a moment longer then follows after them.
Olive turns back to the bench. The more energy she puts into the meal the less it comes together. She has a casserole in the oven and pieces of kumara to bake. She chops the cauliflower into small portions and all the while she is aware of time passing by. It is dark outside now. Pots boil over onto the elements and the steam rising from the oven door smells of burning fat.
After an hour the kumara are still hard. Olive lifts the casserole out and prods at the chunks of meat. They are stringy and grey. She pokes one piece with the sharp end of a knife and thin blood runs out. The carrots have cooked to a mush. She puts the dish back in the oven.
Jim arrives home. "Hello," he says walking straight through into the lounge.
Olive assembles ingredients for a blue-vein dressing to add to the cauliflower. Her breath is short and shallow as she works.
The cheese when it's unwrapped is wet and unpleasantly pungent. Small crystals have formed in the blue areas. Lifting the block she bites into one end and they crunch delicately between her teeth.
The clock shows six-thirty. It is too late. There is no time to go out for more. She crumbles the cheese into a bowl.
Jean and the twins burst into the room. The whole three of them are laughing and talking.
'Look at this.' A string of jet beads drips from Jean's hand. Glossy pieces of stone click together.
'They're beautiful,' says Olive.
The polish is so high that light points are clear white spots on each bead. White dots on ebony. They swing and blaze out from Jean's fingers.
'They're new,' she says. 'I bought them today.'
Olive holds the beads and feels them heavy and cold.

They touch on a dream of some sort.

'Wake up!' Heather shouts. 'Where have you gone to?'

'Ah, nowhere.'

By the time Olive turns back to the stove the cauliflower has boiled dry and the mushrooms have shrunk. Sweat prickles her brow and her hands clench and unclench. She grabs the pots away and puts them on the bench behind.

The casserole is drab and colourless. Olive serves the food at the table and the meal begins.

'I don't know what happened with the meat,' she says. 'It usually comes out better than this.'

'It sure does,' Ruth says dipping a piece of kumara into the gravy.

'It's my usual recipe. I'm sorry.'

'Yes, well,' says Jim.

Cauliflower is left congealing on every plate. Heather stabs a floweret and lifts it to her nose. 'The casserole's all right,' she says. 'But this stuff is appalling. Christ, it's bad.'

'How come it's blue?'

'It's blue-vein dressing. I've made it before.'

'But it's not usually so blue. It's not usually blue at all.'

'Perhaps the cheese was off?'

'No, it's the cauli,' Ruth says. 'It's sulphurous.'

'Well, I'm very sorry. The pudding should be nice.'

Olive takes the plates into the kitchen and scrapes them into the compost bucket. Bright voices and laughter float in from the other room.

She rinses the dishes and stacks them, then leans on the bench. She gazes absently into the sink. A single mushroom stalk lies near the plughole. One end is clean and the other is splayed. It seems the most solitary thing she has ever seen.

She turns her right hand palm up. The bloodstain is deep and red in the hard kitchen light.

Unexpectedly her mouth opens. 'I'm unhappy!' she shouts.

A peel of laughter reaches through, then Ruth's raised voice. 'Can't hear you,' she cries.

'I can't even cook anymore.'

'What?'

'For Christ's sake, I'm not happy.' Her face burns red. Both hands press to her cheeks.

In the other room the conversation is unbroken.

Opening the oven door she takes a dish of apple crumble out. She carries it into the dining room. The dish burns through the cloth to her hands. Putting it down quickly she steps back.

'We can't hear you through the wall.'

'What did you say?'

'I've burnt my hand.'

'Run cold water on it.'

'Yes.'

'Go on then.'

Olive pulls her chair back and sits down.

'You're still dragging your leg.'

'My leg's fine.'

'Crumble, is it?'

Heather takes a spoon and stabs the pudding. She licks the spoon clean. 'Mm, it's edible all right.'

Steam rises through the vent.

'The cream's a bit runny,' Olive says. 'It wouldn't whip properly.'

'It's half-whipped anyway.'

'It'll do.'

'As long as there's plenty of it.' Jim spoons cream onto his serving and it melts and runs across the hot apple.

'Perhaps it was too fresh,' says Olive.

Jean's lips tighten. 'It's not cream that won't whip when it's fresh. It's eggs.'

Turning her head from the table Olive shuts her eyes. The flock of silver birds fly by. They shine and glint with the evening sunlight. They spin in pure air high above the roofs. A blue sky, deep as black. The sun is setting.

She opens her eyes and the room seems brighter than it was previously. The smell of apple crumble is wholesome and sweet. Her own serving is barely touched.

She looks at the faces on either side. Her daughters profiles are strong. Teeth flash white between plump lips.

Jim builds a pyramid of twigs in the lounge fireplace. Olive pulls the curtains.

Ruth comes in waving a piece of paper in one hand. 'Where did this come from?'

She holds the hibiscus painting.

'Where did you get it?' Olive cries.

Ruth spins at the sound of her voice. 'What's the matter?'

'Where was it?'

'The attic room, why?'

Jean stretches a hand and Ruth passes the painting.

'Who did it?'

'I did,' Olive says.

'You did?'

'Some weeks ago.'

'Jesus,' says Heather. 'It's really good.'

Jim puts pine sections into the fire. The bark is slow to ignite.

'I told your mother that.'

'I didn't know you could draw.'

'It's a painting.'

'Well, I didn't know you could paint.'

'Nor did we,' the twins say. 'It's so real.'

'Yes,' Olive says. 'I don't like it too much.'

'I'll have it,' says Ruth.

'Please do.'

'You should take up painting.'

'I've done a few things.'

'What else?'

Olive holds her hands out to the fire and turns them in the heat. 'I'll show you,' she says.

Jim flicks the television switch and static crackles into the room.

Ruth and Heather and Jean follow Olive up the narrow stairway.

'Pooh,' Jean says. 'The room stinks.'

'Does it?'

'Cigarettes. I swear I can smell cigarettes.'

'I can't,' says Olive, looking around. There is no visible evidence.

'It smells like an ashtray.'

Heather points to the wall. 'Did you do those?'
'Yes.'
'Jesus, that's heavy.'
'Yes.'
'Is it supposed to be you?'
'Ah . . . not really.'
'She's a crazy for sure.'
'Can you girls smell cigarettes?' Jeans asks.
'Yeah,' Ruth says. 'Sort of. What else have you done?'
'Well, there's that.'
The flying woman's dark hair floats out and her body is light and free. The colours are clean and vibrant. Olive is overwhelmed by the beauty.
'Nah, don't like it,' says Heather.
'It's a bit basic.'
'Basic, is that how you see it?'
'Well, it's not exactly realistic.'
'I didn't mean it to be.'
'Her feet are too big.'
'Yeah. She's out of proportion.'
'Has she fallen from an aeroplane?'
'Or was she pushed?'
'I like it,' Olive says.
'Take a deep breath,' Jean says. 'It really does smell.'
'Yeah, well it does a bit. What else have you done?'
'That's all to date.'
'What about that sea? Is it a print?'
'I bought it. Do you like it?'
All three answer at once. 'No,' they say.
'We'll stick to the hibiscus,' Ruth says. 'It's good.'
'Do some more like that.'
'I'd like to do some more like the flying one.'
'Nah.'
'You could get into book illustration or anything doing stuff like those flowers.'
'I don't want to get into book illustration or anything.'
'Olive, you are so negative.'
'Let's go downstairs. The fire will be burning by now.'
'I'll come up here in the morning,' says Jean more kindly. 'And air the room.'

CHAPTER NINE

THE MORNING IS Saturday. The twins knock on the bedroom door but without waiting for a reply kick it open and bound in. Heather has the teapot and cups and saucers on a tray.

'Rise and shine,' she cries.

'Cup of tea.'

Jim grumbles. 'It's too early,' he says, moving down in the bed.

'We're starting on the garden.'

'It's in a state.'

'Speak to your mother about that.' He pulls a pillow down and his face disappears.

Olive sits up against the headboard. Ruth passes a full cup of tea and she takes it with both hands. Her cup tilts and tea slops into the saucer.

Heather pulls the blind cord and slats of bamboo roll upwards. The room is filled with cool light.

'Leave it,' says Olive.

The blind clatters down and the room is muted as before.

'No, not the blind. The garden. Leave the garden for now.'

'Nah. We're mentally prepared.'

The blind shoots up again, showing early blue sky.

'It's too cold,' says Olive.

'We'll soon warm up.'

They leave the room and a few minutes later the back door slams shut.

Olive puts her cup of tea aside and rises from the bed. She pulls on her old tartan trousers and a thick shirt. Jim seems to have gone back to sleep.

Shutting the door quietly behind her, she joins Heather

and Ruth in the garden.

They are pulling long strands of wandering jew from beneath the hydrangeas and throwing them onto the lawn.

'Oh dear,' Olive says.

'What?'

'I quite liked it all overgrown down here.'

'Bullshit. It's untidy.'

'Ah well, it's quite pretty all green.'

'It's weeds.'

'Yes, but while the hydrangeas are bare.'

They snort and clouds of steam issue from their mouths into the cold. Olive thinks with longing of her cigarettes hidden in the attic room. Her hands rub together.

She sets off to wander around while behind her the twins rip furiously at the weeds. The garden has become a dismal place. The flowerbeds are thick with weeds and the lawn is damp and patchy. The avocado droops like rubber and the few remaining leaves are wet and hanging.

After a week the fish pie is still unchanged in its dish at the orchard gate. The potato is flecked with green parsley and the fish is a layer of pink and grey.

The dish is still three-quarters full. Nothing has fed here. No animal has partaken, nor any insect.

Olive glances across at the twins. Their voices are a low murmur as they pull and toss the weeds.

Scooping the dish up, Olive hurries into the orchard. She looks from left to right in search of a place to conceal it. Fallen leaves make a damp carpet beneath the avocado. Clearing an area with the toe of her gumboot she deposits the fish pie and covers it with the leaves.

She hurries back through the orchard, pulling the gate shut behind her. Even the solid wood of the gate is slimy to the touch. It leaves a green smear on her hand.

The hydrangeas are exposed now. They are a row of white sticks rising up from bare soil. The wandering jew is piled into a mound on the lawn.

Heather and Ruth stretch and bend and rub their hands on their legs. 'Next?' they say.

'Next what?'

'Flowerbeds or the orchard?'

'Come in for breakfast now.'
'Nah.'
'Bacon and eggs.'
'We're working up a decent appetite.'
Olive joins them in the flowerbeds. 'Be careful,' she says. 'I've put bulbs in.'
In cold earth the weeds are tenacious. Some break off at ground level and others bring great clods of soil up with their roots.
Ruth takes the hoe and begins chopping over the weeded area.
'I don't think you should, dear,' says Olive. 'The bulbs should be coming up.'
'I can't see any yet.'
'They should be up soon.'
Ruth drops the hoe onto the lawn and goes back to working with her hands. When the bed is finished they step back.
Although the weeded areas are clean, to Olive's eye there is no improvement. The weeds at least were green.
'It's winter,' she says. 'Things stop in winter.'
'No excuse.' Ruth walks away.
Heather pushes the orchard gate open. 'We should chop that tree down.'
Olive is immediately cold. The chill moves up her legs and down from above. Ice forms in the middle. 'It'll recover in the spring,' she cries.
'Nah, it won't.'
'It's stuffed.'
'You're not to touch it.'
'Jesus.' Ruth looks back at Olive. 'It was just a suggestion.'
'Oh, I am sorry,' says Olive. 'But I don't want it touched.'
'All right. Got the message.'
'I'm so cold. I'll have to go in.'
Heather calls from the other side of the orchard. Her tracksuit is bright red amongst the grey trunks. She moves forward and then stops.
'What's the matter?'
'Ooh, yuk,' she says. 'I don't believe it.'

'What is it?'

She turns around and the dish of fish pie waves in her hand. 'What is this crap?'

'It's a smoked fish pie.'

'It's absolutely disgusting.' The dish drops from her hand and rolls over and over, ending on its side. The food remains stuck in the same position.

Olive can see several brown leaves where they are plastered across. 'Ahh,' she says.

'What's it doing in the orchard?'

'It's for a cat.'

'What cat?'

'Wild cats live in the garden, you know.'

'They mightn't find it, buried like that.'

'Just leave it where it is, Heather. A cat will get it.'

'Don't worry,' she says. 'I'm not taking it anywhere.'

Olive walks to the end of the garden path, then beyond that. She follows the line of tall trees on the boundary. Her gumboots sink into the lawn.

In the corner of the property where the rimu stands, the shadow is densest. She moves forward until she is enveloped by it. Clumps of toadstools have appeared. They grow at the base of the tree and further back near the wall. Rounded tops bulge straight up out of the soil.

As Olive looks she sees more and more of them. They are beige and fleshy.

It seems they are everywhere.

Jean appears at the breakfast table in an acid-pink dress. Her eyelids are semicircles of the same colour and gold discs swing from her ears.

'You're looking very nice,' Jim says.

She drops saccharin into a cup of black coffee and smiles all around the table.

Olive looks down at her plate. There is nothing on it.

The twins eat two servings of bacon and eggs and start on the toast. They spread the slices with generous quantities of butter.

'Ah, food.' Ruth pours marmalade straight from the jar.

'We could go for a drive,' Jim says. 'It looks like a good

day for a drive.'

Jean looks at Olive and the lines stretch around her lips. 'You could wear your nice new clothes,' she says.

Taking a piece of toast, Olive cuts it into quarters. She places the knife on the side of her plate. 'You can cut toast into triangles or squares,' she says.

'What new clothes?' Ruth asks.

'Well, they're not exactly new now,' says Jean. 'But she hasn't worn them yet. There's a skirt and a jacket and a beautiful silk blouse. It's that heavy silk. It's lovely. I had to take them back to the shop for your mother and get smaller sizes. She's too thin.'

'Show us.'

Olive bites her toast and chews slowly.

'Wear them,' Jim says. 'I've not even seen you in them yet.'

'All right, all right.'

'As for those trousers. Well,' says Jean. 'Tartan trousers.'

'Very nice,' Heather says. 'The baggy look. It's all the rage.'

'The no-arse look.'

'They look like jodhpurs.'

'I've been gardening. I only wear them around the house.'

Since exchanging the clothes Olive has lost even more weight. The jacket bags around her chest and the skirt sits low on her waist.

'Don't worry,' says Jean. 'We can take the waistband in. I do hope you're not ill.'

'Of course I'm not ill.' Olive stands in front of the long mirror. 'I'm ready to go.'

'You should go to the doctor.'

'What for?'

'You know why. You're too thin and you limp and you've got a nervous twitch in your eye. You can't wear those shoes.'

'Why not?'

'They don't match.'

'They're fine.'

'Look good for Jim. Just this once. Make an effort. You'll feel better if you do.'

The twins come into the bedroom. 'Hey, you look good.'
'Turn around.'
'Skin and bones.'
'What's happened to your chest, though?'
'It's gone concave,' Ruth says.
'It's not really. It's just that her posture is bad.'
'We'll do your hair.'
'I don't want it done.'
'It would suit you more brushed back. And curled around like this.'
'I'll get my hairspray,' Jean says.
'And pink lipstick. Pink looks good with cream.'
'I don't feel comfortable in cream. All these pale colours. I like dark colours.'
Jean rolls her eyes. 'Cheerful colours like black. Hold on, I'll be back in a jiff.'
Olive sits on the bed and smooths the suit down. The silk blouse is slippery and cold on her skin.
Ruth brushes her hair back from behind. She pulls and twists the strands and Heather follows with the hairspray. The heavy perfume is suffocating.
When they have finished Ruth applies make-up to her face. Olive keeps her eyes closed.
'There you go,' Heather says.
The face that stares back from the bedroom mirror isn't her own but a sophisticated copy of it. Her skin is matt where the foundation has dried and her lips shine glossy pink. Her eyelids are coloured with soft brown shades.
But her eyes below are incongruous. They are dark with despair. Looking out through eyes like these, she thinks. Ahh.
She smiles at the mirror but the smile is hollow and sad. Her gaze drops to the floor.
Her tartan trousers are a small dark bundle in the corner. The blue tip of a handkerchief protrudes from a pocket. Olive pulls it out and rolls it in a ball. She holds it tight in her hand.
'Oh boy,' Jim says. 'You've done a great job, girls.' He circles Olive looking her up and down. 'Fantastic.'
She stuffs the handkerchief into her jacket pocket and

tries not to cry.

Olive sits in the back of the car with Heather and Ruth. Kicking her tight shoes off she settles down into the seat. She looks out the window but sees little.

After a time the road west climbs into the foothills of the Waitakere Ranges and the houses are spaced further and further apart. Bush grows in between. The tarseal is replaced by loose metal and the car slows.

As the houses drop back Olive's feelings of despondency lift. 'It's so nice to see bush,' she says.

'Oh good, you're speaking again, are you?' Jim steers sharply into a corner. Stones and dust spray out from the tyres.

The road snakes and twists for some time. At the top of the incline he pulls over onto the shoulder of the road.

Far below, the city stretches in a grid of roads and buildings. Green volcanic hills thrust up here and there and the harbour is a wide ribbon of blue. Spanning it small but clear in the distance is the arc of the harbour bridge.

Jim flicks the ignition key. The motor purrs into life again and the car moves off.

The smell of bush reaches in. Trees grow on either side. Parts of the road are misty with low cloud. The smell is of water and earth.

A van overtakes and speeds ahead.

'A maniac,' Ruth says.

The conversation is sporadic.

On the far side of the ranges the land plunges steeply. Jim changes down a gear and then another. They drive slowly down to the coast. At the bottom the road levels out.

Cliffs rise into hills on either side. The low manuka growth is stunted and the higher peaks are hidden in cloud.

The beach is an undulating spread of black sand running down flat at the watermark. The sea is a fury of white. The air is filled with the sound of its thunder. Massive waves cut across each other and crash.

Olive is made speechless by the beauty.

'Jesus,' Jim says. 'What a godforsaken spot.'

'Miserable,' says Jean.
'Hey no, it's great,' says Ruth.
'Shall we walk down to the sea?'
'Nah.'
'Nah.'
'It's too cold.'

Ruth takes a block of chocolate from her bag and peels the wrapper back. 'Who's for chocolate?' she strips off the foil.

The tablet breaks down into strips and then squares in her hands. Peanuts show clumped on the underside of each piece as she passes them around.

They stare from the windows. Sand blows across the dunes while the sea pounds the beach. The towering waves are white with foam and sheets of spray float onto the cliffs.

But there is another movement on the beach. Something follows the waves as they recede and rushes back as a new one explodes on the shore.

'Can you see something right down near the water?' asks Olive.

'The twins lean forward. 'No,' they say. 'It's too far away to see.'

'Just there where the waves come up on the sand. Look see.'

'What sort of something?'

'I don't know.'

'Nothing there,' says Jim.

But again there is a movement. Then a small shape is tossed upwards from the middle. For a second it glints silver.

'Look!' she says.

Four heads turn but there is nothing.

When it happens again Olive has time to see the vee of a bird's split tail. The silver birds, she thinks with astonishment. Here on the coast.

She opens the car door and bitter air rushes in.

'Jesus, shut the door.'

'I'd like to walk,' she says.

'Quick, shut the door.'

'I'll just walk down to the sea and back.'
'It's too bloody cold.'
'You'll freeze.'
'You can't walk in the sand in those shoes, Olive. You'll ruin your shoes.'
'I'll just walk on the hard bits.'
'Man, you're crazy,' says Ruth.
Olive bites through the piece of chocolate in her mouth and the taste is sweet. She steps from the car and shuts the door behind her.
Wind cuts through the thin fabric of her jacket and her hair blows down around her ears. With each step her heels stab into the sand and drag at her feet. She presses on.
The birds have moved further along the beach. They are small dark shapes leaping up and floating back down onto the sand.
'Wait, wait!' Ripping the shoes from her feet Olive runs in her stockings.
After a few steps she stops and looks back to the car. Three faces are pale discs turned towards her. In the driver's seat Jim stares straight ahead.
She waves. No movement in the car indicates a reply.
The birds are hopping and jumping. Olive rushes over the loose sand. Her feet slide and sink in and now she's on the hard. This area has been packed down by the sea.
The waves swell high and green. Rising higher and higher until they tremble and crash. Foam and spray fly into the air. Swift tongues of water run up onto the sand.
Olive runs along parallel to the breaking waves. Her shoes swing in her hand. Air freezes in her lungs and she's gasping for new breath.
She slows and stops near the birds. They show little sign of alarm. Her breath draws in. These are birds like no others.
She glances around. Sand dunes block the car from sight and the coast is deserted.
She turns back to the birds. The silver birds. And yet one of them is emerald green. It is the most vivid colour. There are sixteen silver birds and one of green. Why one of green?

Even in this place where the light is dulled by cloud and the sand is sullen as charcoal they are iridescent.

Olive inches forward and as she moves they do likewise so the separating distance remains unchanged.

She stops again. Even at this distance she is close enough to see the light-spots shine on the rounds of their eyes and to notice the immaculate shafts and barbs of their feathers. Each feather fits perfectly into the next, as if crafted from the finest silver.

As they leap from the sand their wings open and spread and soft down beneath ruffles in the wind.

With absolute precision, they hop down towards the ocean as the water sucks back and fling themselves skywards when a fresh wave surges onto the beach.

Each new wave smooths the imprints of their feet away then the water drags back and they mark the sand afresh.

Olive rubs her arms against the cold and curls her toes. She pushes the wind-blown hair off her face.

On this wild beach the emerald bird has the hue of a rare tropical fruit. Scarcely able to look, she turns to the sea.

A huge wave forms into a ridge. Spray whips from the crest as it moves towards the beach. For a brief moment it seems to pause. The wall of water is translucent green, streaked with brown where kelp strands ride. A shudder runs along its length and then it is curving and breaking in a fury of white. Salt is sharp in the air.

Water surges up onto the beach. Cross-currents meet and form small waves of their own. The ripples flatten and it drains away.

Running down onto the wet sand, Olive follows the wave out. The birds spiral and duck around her feet. Silver flashes past her face.

Another wave swells for the race into shore. It is gaining speed now. With the water almost upon her, Olive turns.

Her footprints are a straight line on the sand and those prints the birds have made are starburst all around. She looks at the patterns and a sound of joy rises in her throat.

The birds rise up in a shining cloud. Their wings brush her hands and face and she runs racing the wave.

Icy water licks her heels and climbs higher, splashing onto her clothes. Her feet lift out of the foam and disappear again until at last the water turns and drains back.

Olive stands there panting. A strand of seaweed lies across the toes of her left foot. Her stockings cling like skin where they are wet and clusters of ladders run up from the soles and over her ankles.

She looks at the feet with surprise as if they aren't her own. Long bones run down the length of them. Wet on the sand they seem strong and good.

The birds don't come back to land this time. Forming a circle in the air they take on the familiar pattern of flight. They are turning and weaving around and around.

Higher and higher they spin until they are specks in the sky and the emerald bird is indistinguishable from the rest.

Why one bird of green? Such a colour.

A high wave washes up cold around Olive's feet and her eyes drop. A single fragment of white shell tumbles in the water.

Bending forward, she picks it up and wipes it dry on her jacket. The spine is thick and strong and curved like a crescent moon. One side is corrugated with sweeping lines and the other side is marble smooth. She drops it into her pocket.

Olive begins to walk back along the beach. The birds are only visible as a faint dark mass now. As she watches, a lower bank of cloud moves across the sky and they are gone.

A jutting rock face forms the end of the beach. There is a small stream running alongside it on its way to the sea.

Olive leaves the hard sand and walks up onto the dry. It clings to her wet stockings and coats them with a gritty black pile.

The car comes into view. All four faces are turned towards her as she struggles through the soft drifts.

Her stomach tightens and she grips the shell in her pocket so the edge is sharp on her palm. The pain of it is good.

The stream borders the carpark on one side. Stepping down into the raw water Olive stands there watching the sand wash away from her ankles.

Dropping her shoes on the bank she pushes her feet into them one at a time and steps awkwardly to the car. The soles squeak as she moves.

A door opens and Jean springs out. 'My God, Olive!' she screams. 'What happened?'

'Nothing.'

'Nothing! How can you say nothing? Look at you, you've ruined your clothes! You're soaked through, you'll get pneumonia!'

'I'm fine, thank you.'

'You were gone for ages. What happened to your feet?' Turning to the car she flings up her arms.

'Ha ha ha,' Heather and Ruth laugh, slapping their knees in the back seat. Their torsos jerk back and forwards.

Jim remains still but his jaw is tight with anger.

Olive climbs into the car and settles next to the twins.

'Ha, they're in shreds.' Ruth pokes a finger into a hole in Olive's stockings. 'Ha ha,' she roars. 'If you pulled that hole there and that hole there the whole leg would break in half.'

'Can I do it?' says Heather.

'No.'

'Did you tap dance on the rocks in your stockings?'

'Yes,' Olive says.

'What a scream.' Tears roll down their cheeks.

'You've ruined those shoes,' says Jean, turning around in the front seat.

'They're all right.'

'They're Spanish leather, aren't they?' asks Jim.

'Ah, Spanish, yes, or maybe they're Italian. I don't know.'

'They'll be ruined.'

'I've only ruined my pantyhose.'

'What did you do?'

'I just went for a walk.'

'I hope nobody saw you,' Jean says.

'There wasn't a soul in sight.'

'Are you cold?'

'No.'

'Your teeth are chattering.'

'They're doing it by themselves.'

'Christ almighty.' Heather clicks her own teeth in exaggerated imitation.

The twins start up again. 'Ha ha ha,' they roar.

Jim flicks the ignition and backs out of the parking area. He accelerates up the road. Jean stares straight ahead beside him. The lacquered waves of her hair are rigid as the car lurches.

Olive turns for a last glimpse of the sea. Framed between two hills, it is a white triangle running back into grey. The shore is a black strip.

Slipping the shoes off, she wriggles her toes. They are cold and quite numb. Now sitting side by side on the carpeted floor of the car they seem pathetic and ugly. They are quite without power.

The road climbs into the hills and cloud is all around.

The car turns into the driveway. Olive climbs out stiffly and holds the door for the twins.

A small ginger cat squeezes through a bush and springs onto the lawn.

'Look, a cat,' Ruth says.

Licking a paw it rolls over on the grass. A white line runs down one side of its neck and spreads across its belly.

Olive touches the soft fur and the cat curls around her hand, biting into her thumb. 'I don't know whose it is,' she says. 'I saw it on the footpath once before.'

She straightens and the cat rubs on her ankles.

Jim walks across the veranda to the front door. His key turns in the lock and he steps aside to let Jean and the twins through.

'You'd better change,' he says wearily, disappearing into the house.

Olive scoops the cat up and carries it down the side path to the back garden. It starts to purr and its body vibrates in her arms.

The orchard gate swings open on its hinges. Stepping past, she walks down between the plum tree and the fig and then pauses.

In front of the avocado the fish pie dish lies on its side as it was left in the morning.

'Fish pie,' she says.

The cat stretches up until its face pushes on her chin. Kneeling down, she puts it beside the dish.

'Ah, lovely tempting fish pie,' she whispers.

Oblivious, the cat flops over on its back in the grass and looks up at the sky. Sparrows chirp in the branches of the fig.

Olive turns the animal around and gently pushes its face down. The little body stiffens in her hands. The cat smells the food and its tail thickens like a brush then it's off running up the slope of the orchard.

'Puss puss,' Olive calls.

The cat continues. At the edge of the orchard it dives into a clump of arum lilies. Against the long green leaves its tail is a crooked orange line. White lilies shake on their stalks as the cat weaves through the plants.

Olive stands staring. The flowers are still again, but the protruding yellow stamens continue to tremble. Whether it is from the cat or from a movement of their own, it is difficult to tell.

As she is dressing for bed Olive turns, startled by the feeling of another person in the room. Her own image moves on the mirror.

Quickly she looks away and pulls the nightdress down over her head, then just as swiftly lifts it off again. It drops from her hand to the floor.

Jim's voice and female laughter sound and fade in another room.

Olive looks to the long mirror. The face reflected there is afraid and the body is bent in on itself in an attitude of defence. One arm crosses her naked chest and the other is around her waist. Her belly is a tiny bowl between jutting pelvic bones. Below it the triangle of pubic hair is black. On her shrunken body it looks too dark.

Her arm falls away from her breasts. They are empty and low on her chest and between them ridges of rib run together and meet.

So thin, she thinks. The body is unfamiliar. It is the figure of a stranger.

'Olive,' she says and the dark eyes stare and blink.

Voices swell and footsteps clatter in the hall. She scrambles back into the nightdress and presses the light switch.

It is dark in the room now. Pencils of moonlight glow between the slats of the bamboo blind. Olive rolls it up and the moon is round and pale blue.

'Lunar light,' she says and within moments is asleep.

At some stage during the night words sound in her ears and she awakens.

'I do hope you're not ill.'

Olive's eyes open wide in the dark. Jim is stretched out beside her in bed now but he sleeps heavily. Beyond the regular sounds of his breath the house is still.

'I do hope you're not ill.' They were Jean's words. Fingering the new skirt where it was loose on her waist, Jean had said it. What did she mean?

Sweat breaks out on Olive's hands although the night is cool. She pulls herself upright in the bed.

The blind is down again and the room is inky. The big vase is a black circle on the dressing table.

Her eyes strain and the sweat moves up her arms and down her back. A fever, she thinks.

A car drives up the street and the sound of its motor is loud in the night. It roars. Jim is undisturbed.

'I hope you're not ill.' Olive tosses in the bed.

Heather and Ruth appear at the bedroom door in the morning. They both wear long white tee-shirts. Their legs are bare. 'Surprise,' they sing, bounding from one side of the room to the other.

'White knickers,' Jim says.

'They are not. They're pink.'

'White.'

'Pink.'

'Surprise,' Heather shouts. Her arm flashes from behind her back. Olive's purse is in her hand. The purse she had dropped for the Maori girl.

Olive jumps in the bed. 'Where did you get that from?' she cries.

'Ooh, easy, easy.'

'Where was it?'

'You lost it.'

Olive holds her hand out. 'Who said I lost it?'

'Yuk, that blotch.'

'You said it was a liver spot.'

'It's not going away.'

'You said it wouldn't.'

'No, it won't.'

'Who said I lost it?'

'Lost what?'

'My purse.'

'Jean said you lost it at the dairy.'

'Ah, did she?'

'I want my breakfast in bed,' Jim says. 'It's Sunday, isn't it?'

Ruth unzips the purse and fingers through the various compartments. 'Your money's gone,' she says.

'Can I have it?'

'You've been ripped off.'

'How much was in it?'

'Not much. Please pass it here.'

'Hey, it's full of crap.'

'Take it away,' Jim says. 'I'll have an omelet with tomato and onion and two pieces of toast. And some sort of juice. Cold orange juice, I think.'

Ruth turns the purse upside down and shakes it. Tiny shapes flash in the air as scraps of paper flutter to the floor. Fragments spiral in front of the girls' brown legs.

Olive leaps from the bed. The paper shapes have settled on the carpet and she is on her knees scraping them up into her hands.

'No, make that three pieces of toast.'

'Give me that purse!' Olive shouts.

'We have a mad woman on our hands.' Ruth throws the purse down.

She and Heather jump onto the bed and begin thumping

Jim with the pillows.

'With melted butter!' he cries. The pillows puff down on his head.

'Where did you find it?' Olive asks.

'No butter for you.'

'Oozing and dripping,' Jim says.

'Where did you find the purse?'

'Cholesterol, cholesterol,' they sing.

'Where, where?'

'In the letterbox. Sticking out of the letterbox,' Heather says. 'Buttery toast all dripping and buttery.'

Olive pushes the pieces of paper back into the purse. Standing up, she leaves the room. She steps through the bathroom door and locks it behind.

Kneeling on the floor she spreads the scraps out on the cold tiles. They are birds. Small pictures of birds cut from magazines. There are pigeons and sparrows and a turquoise kingfisher.

Olive examines every piece. The paper is porous and the shapes are roughly cut or ripped. Some are from photographs and others have been drawn. She recognizes a dove with half-folded wings from a magazine advertisement. It is the trademark of a cleaning product.

Scooping them into her hands again she stands up and lets them fall. Against the clinical white walls the flickering shapes are even brighter. They descend in a gay swirling mist.

One lands in a drop of water on the handbasin. Olive slides it along with her finger. Although damp, the picture can still be clearly seen. It is a female sparrow.

Its body faces the camera and its head is turned to the left. The bird's eye is bright and keen.

Olive leaves the breakfast things and goes out into the garden. Entering the gloomy space beneath the rimu she reaches into her pocket for a cigarette. She lights it and takes a long breath, then another. The smoke blows upwards. Milky rivers of it twist around the branches.

Toadstools bloom in pulpy clumps in leaf mould at the base of the tree. Are there even more today? They are thick and unpleasantly pink.

A door slams at the house and two pairs of feet appear on the back steps. Olive watches through a gap in the tree. She can hear voices now.

Pushing her cigarette into the ground she covers the butt with loose soil. She moves further back beneath the cover of the rimu.

Trapped by a weeping canopy of foliage the cigarette smoke is a white pall. Can they see it leaking through into the clean air? Can they smell it? It's too late to do anything now.

Jean and Heather are on the garden path. Only their feet and legs are visible but their voices are clear. Heather's socks are orange and her sandshoes are white. The orange and white comes closer and closer then stops.

'She's slipped badly,' Jean says.

'She's just slack.' Heather steps out to the clothesline and her hands appear plucking pegs. Something pink is flung across the line.

'It's more than that.'

Olive is frozen. On the other side of the trailing rimu branches one shoe taps on the path. Orange and white. Up and down.

'Ruth and I have given up.'

'She doesn't look after herself. She doesn't do her hair or bother with her face.' Jean's voice is shrill. 'She won't even cook a decent meal. She's a good cook. You know that.'

'I know.'

'Your poor father.'

'He's getting pretty sick of it.'

'Sick of it!' Jean shrieks. 'I should think he would be. Look at the performance yesterday. She's ruined those clothes.'

'A drycleaner might be able to fix them up.'

'That's not the point.'

'No.'

'I feel I should stay, Heather. Until she makes some sort of effort. Look at the place, dear. Our mother would turn in her grave.'

'What nail polish is that?' Heather asks.
'Peach dream.'
'Peach dream.' The white shoe taps up and down.
'It's more apricot, really.'
'It's great.'
'Jim rang and asked me to keep an eye on your mother. You know that, don't you dear?'
'Yeah, Dad said.'
Olive's teeth crack together and her body lurches. She leans against the tree. Oh Christ.
'Your father's a tolerant man.'
'There's not a hell of a lot you can do, you know. If she won't help herself, nobody else can.'
'I know. But I'll stay and do what I can.'
'Can I try your nail polish?'
'Of course. You girls have such lovely strong nails.'
'This one broke off at work. I stuck it back on with superglue.'
'Did you really? You'd never know.'
The orange socks stride off and Jean's heels click on the path.
Near the orchard gate they stop again and snatches of their conversation drift down to the bottom of the garden. Their heads are visible now. Jean's hands fly into the air in a gesture of outrage. Columns of rings glint gold and white on her fingers.
They move slowly away. Climbing the back stairs they re-enter the house. The door bangs shut behind them.
Olive draws another cigarette from the packet. Her fingers shake violently. Three matches flick to the ground before she is able to light it from the burning tip of the fourth. Smoke winds upwards.
Against her cheek the rimu bark is rough and cool. A lonely wind stirs the weeping branches and Olive draws on the cigarette. 'Ahh,' she says.
A decision presses down. What options are there? She can't see any at all.
The trunk sways gently scraping her face and it seems there is no longer time to delay. I have to decide. Her right eye flutters at the thought.

CHAPTER TEN

OLIVE CHOOSES THREE arum lilies and several leaves. Two of the flowers are full and open and the third is a bud. Cutting through the fleshy stalks, she shakes them gently. Dew spins off.

She takes them up the stairs and into the house. The attic room is cold. Little light reflects from the rooftops today and the harbour is grey frosted glass. A thin mist hovers across the far side.

Olive sets paper and paints on the table. She arranges the lilies in a jar then steps back to view them.

The green of the stalks extends onto the base of the flowers. Fine lines of this colour reach up and fade. Green blends into white. A single yellow stamen points up from the centre of each flower. The sides and tips are coated with a powdery white.

The leaves are green and curving. Their lines and those of the lilies are simple and clean.

She draws them in pencil. Each line is precise. She takes care to represent them as they are to be seen.

When the drawing is complete she mixes the paints. Blue and yellow blend together into green. She squeezes white and yellow straight from the tubes.

Olive works at filling in the first lily. She shades the colour down one side and deep into the throat.

The door handle turns and Jean is in the room. 'What are you doing?' she says. 'Lovely. Funeral lilies.'

'Funeral lilies?'

'That's what they're called.'

'Arum lilies.'

'No, funeral. People take them to funerals. They used

to, anyway.' She leans over the paper. 'Hence the name.' The jet beads swing out glinting and black from her throat.

'I've never heard them called that.' Olive rinses her brush in a jar of water and it hits the glass with a single high clink.

'Very good,' says Jean.

One white lily stands out alive on the flat plane of paper. There is a gap where the stamen will be.

Olive coats her brush with yellow paint but stands there letting it dry.

'I like the bud,' she says. 'Look how it twists around.'

'It's nearly lunch-time.'

'Look at those lines! Look how it's furled!'

'Lunch-time, Olive.'

'What's that?'

'You know. Time to eat something. Most people eat in the middle of the day.'

'I didn't realise it was that late.'

'You've been up here for several hours.'

'Have I really?'

'Is it that you just have no appetite, or what?'

'Ah, I don't know. It's just that I hadn't thought about it.'

Olive washes the brush and reloads it with green. She draws it up the stalk.

'You just don't eat, Olive. I'm worried about your health. I wish you'd see the doctor.'

'I'm fine.'

'Our mother got very thin like you.

'Did she?'

'Yes, she did at the end. Then she died.'

'Well I'm not dying, I'm sure.'

'She had cancer.'

'Cancer?'

'That's what she died of.'

A chill moves the brush in Olive's hand and a vein drops in the middle of a leaf where it should run straight. 'Oh dear,' she says.

'You haven't been yourself, you know that.'

Olive takes a finer brush and repairs the area. 'I know,'

she says at last. 'I've been very unhappy. It's not an easy time for a woman, but I've been thinking it through and I'm prepared to make an effort now. I'll be all right.'

'Do you really mean that?'

Olive looks at Jean's square face. Her eyes are pale.

'I do. I'm sorry, I know it's been a bit hard but I'll be okay now.'

Jean squints her eyes and her lips stretch. 'You've no idea how glad I am to hear you being positive for a change,' she says. 'You make yourself very unhappy, you know that, don't you?'

'Yes.' A dark green line runs away from the tip of her brush. It shades the side of a stalk.

'All you need to do is eat more and take greater pains with your appearance. You'd feel a lot better.'

'Yes.'

'And get out and about.'

'Yes.'

'It does you no good to stay in the house such a lot.'

'No.'

'I'm going out shortly myself.'

'Are you going to the hospital to see David?'

'No, I need to buy a new handbag. I'll visit him tomorrow.'

Jean's perfume lingers long after she has left the room. Olive opens the windows. There is a smell of cold salt water in the air.

'Funeral lilies,' she mutters, taking up a new brush.

Furled and green except for the opening lip, the bud comes slowly to life. It leans away from the already rendered flower.

She prepares fresh paint for a leaf and colours the bold outline with a single stroke.

By the middle of the afternoon the work is finished. Olive takes the painting downstairs and pins it above the mantelpiece. Small areas of paint are still wet.

She steps back to look at it. The lilies are astonishingly realistic. They stand out as if freshly plucked.

She is agitated with anger. She shuts her eyes then opens them again and a new surge courses through. The painting is not of her choice, but Jim and Jean will approve of it. Such an exercise is meaningless.

The images in her mind are of hills and valleys. High slopes of raw land reach into a savage sky. It is a primitive and dramatic landscape.

I should be painting that, she thinks. Or bird marks in wet sand. Starbursts showing on a subtle background, or the colour of emerald on grey. Sixteen silver birds and one of green.

'I should be painting the roundness of eggs,' she cries.

Spinning on her heel Olive leaves the room.

Jean has left lunch set on the table. There are two slices of brown bread and cheese on one plate and gherkins and rolled pink ham on another.

Olive eats the cheese and one slice of bread but has little appetite for anything else. Her stomach is quite full.

Taking the two rolls of ham she steps through the back door. She hurls them from the top step out into the garden. The slices of meat unroll and flatten in the air.

'A cat will get it!' she shouts.

There is no response from the garden. The sky is low and grey as if the harbour mist has risen and thickened right across. The colours of the day seem strangely flat.

Olive goes back into the lounge. Standing just inside the doorway she studies the painting. Funeral lilies, she thinks.

In her mind she can see the lilies which grew behind the house of her childhood. The paddock is wet here and grass topped lumps of soil stand up from the mud. The lilies grow along the fence.

Now Olive appears in the picture as well. She is a solitary child moving through the plants in a long brown coat.

There is nothing bright. The colours are strangely flat. The white of these lilies isn't pure so much as sombre.

And through this light it seems that a change has occurred to the painting. Looking at it now, Olive is no longer angry. Her anger has changed into sadness.

Olive takes her shopping bag and leaves the house. She walks slowly up the hill.

Standing outside the butcher-shop window she looks

at the lines of red meat. The trays are decorated with sprigs of parsley and plastic lemons.

The butcher waves through the window. He slaps a piece of meat down.

Pulling the door back she steps into the smell of blood. 'I haven't made my mind up yet,' she says.

She is confused by the different cuts of meat. It is taking too long to decide. Her eyes keep returning to the plastic lemons. They are yellow and shiny and pitted. Some have leaves attached and others are plain.

'Look at this,' the butcher says. A length of meat swings from his hand.

It looks like an organ of some sort. 'What is it?' she says.

'Cancer.'

'What?'

'Cancerous meat. You see the odd tumour from time to time. What would you like today?'

Appalled, Olive turns away. 'I need something for the cat,' she whispers.

'Pardon?'

'The cat.'

'Gravy beef, I suppose.'

'I don't know. I'll come back later,' she says, pushing the door open.

Tempting smells waft out from the delicatessen. Olive waits while the woman grinds coffee behind the counter.

She buys a french loaf already sliced and spread with garlic butter and an asparagus quiche. Spears of asparagus radiate out like spokes from the centre. The woman slides it into a flat box and tucks the lid down.

Olive hurries past the butcher-shop window. The entire meat display seems contaminated. She holds her breath as if the disease is in the very air and still holding it rushes across the street.

Halfway down the hill she stops again. A man in orange overalls is trimming branches from the red hibiscus on the verge.

Olive stands alongside. Unaware, he continues. He pulls the branches down roughly and his saw rips into the bark

and through to the naked wood below.
'Are you from the council?' she asks.
He looks over his shoulder.'That's right,' he says.
White pulp clings to the teeth of the saw in his hand.
Olive walks slowly away.

Jim finishes his quiche. 'I'd love more,' he says. 'It's delicious. The best you've made for a while.'
Olive takes his plate to the oven and cuts another piece.
'Is that enough?' she says.
'That's fine.'
'Jean?'
'No, I mustn't, but it really is very nice.'
'Good.'
'How many eggs did you use?'
'Eggs, ah, five.'
'Five. Well.'
'A definite improvement,' Jim says. His knife sinks into the pie.
'And she did a painting too.'
'A painting?'
'Didn't you see it in the lounge?'
'No. What is it?'
'I did a few lilies.'
Jean springs from the room and returns with the painting. Pins still protrude from the four corners of the paper.
'Hello!' says Jim, reaching out and taking it. He lays it flat on the table. 'Excellent. It's excellent.'
'Aren't they real?'
'Yes, very good. Very real.'
'Look at that drop of dew. I told Olive you could almost flick it off, it looks so real.'
'Mm, it's a very wet drop of dew.' Jim cuts his quiche into neat squares and stabs the nearest one with his fork. 'Good soft egg, this.'
'I put arum lilies on Father's grave,' says Olive. 'Jim, do you remember that?'
'Didn't we buy real flowers?'
'Real flowers? We took crimson roses, but I took arum

lilies as well. They grew on the farm when we were kids.'
'They grow everywhere,' Jean says. 'They're actually weeds.'
'They're beautiful, though.'
Pushing back in his chair, Jim stretches one arm then the other over his head. Black cuff-links glint on his white shirt cuffs. 'Keep up the painting,' he says. 'You could go places.'
Taking the painting, Olive holds it out at arm's length. The mournful flowers fill her vision.
Only two places to go, she thinks. One is up and the other is down. She feels on the very edge. A small slip either way would define the direction.
Ahh. At least pretend it's all right.
Jean is smiling brightly. 'Let's go and see David tomorrow,' she says. 'Shall we?'
'Yes, all right.'
'I'll leave the car for you,' says Jim.

Olive drives into the hospital carpark and pulls into a space.
Jean applies another coat of lipstick. 'I'm not looking forward to this,' she says. At a twist of her fingers the tube of acid pink retreats.
'Let's go.'
'How do I look?'
Olive opens the car door and steps out. 'You're looking good,' she says.
They walk across an area of concrete. Jean pushes a button at the front entrance. A faint bell sounds deep inside the building.
Keys rattle and the front door swings open. A tall stooped man stands there. 'Who do you want to see?' he says.
The room they are shown into seems to be a dining room. A large expanse of green-flecked linoleum is covered with formica tables and chairs.
The only other people are a woman and a small child. They sit at a table in the centre of the room. The child's jacket is imitation sheepskin. Amongst a barren mass of table tops and chair legs the fluffy texture is incongruous.

Jean strides across the room on her high heels. She swings her handbag onto a table near the far wall. 'Come on,' she says.

Olive hurries across.

'How dismal.'

'We're locked in,' Olive whispers.

'It's not us who are locked in, it's them.'

'No, we are as well. He locked the door we came through and he locked that door he went out. We're locked in.'

'Sit down,' says Jean.

'Yes, all right.'

'Don't panic.'

'I don't like it.'

'I think you'll find they'll let us out.'

The child cries and arches her back on the woman's knee. She slides to the floor and stands there on wobbly legs. The woman takes a pink pacifier from a bag and the child draws it into her mouth. The jacket hood falls back from her head and her hair is a soft orange down.

'Dirty things,' Jean says.

'Dirty?'

'Dummies. They're horrible.'

'Look at the child's hair,' Olive whispers. 'It's so lovely.'

'Redhead. Her face will be too white when she's older.'

'He's taking ages.'

'She'll freckle in the sun.'

'I wish he'd come.'

'I suppose they have to fetch him from somewhere.'

'Yes.'

'This place stinks,' says Jean.

'Yes.'

'Cigarette smoke.'

'I can't smell it much.'

'Oh, Olive, you can. It's revolting.'

The door rattles open and a man is allowed through. His head is bandaged. As he draws closer Olive can see that the bandage is in fact a continuous length of toilet paper. It wraps around and around and is secured on one side with strips of sellotape.

He is a tall man and his trousers reach only halfway

down his calves. Between the trouser cuffs and his socks his legs are white and hairy. He approaches the woman and the child.

'My godfathers!' Jean says.

Olive looks at the walls. They are green-grey and bare except for a scarred area near the floor.

'That's toilet paper around his head,' Jean says.

'Shh, he might hear you.'

'Well perhaps someone should tell him.'

The walls stretch right up to the top. The ceiling is the same colour but a shade lighter.

'He's taking so long.'

The man scoops the child up and bounces her on his knee. The woman lights a cigarette and passes it to him. She takes another one from the packet and lights it for herself.

Ash falls into the child's hair. Neither of them make any move to brush it off.

Olive touches the top of her own head as if that will sweep the ash away.

The child stares straight ahead and the plastic ring on her dummy bobs up and down as she sucks.

The door opens and David is stepping through. A group of men crowd behind him to see through the doorway. The door slams in their faces.

David saunters over to the table. It seems to take a long time.

'What are you wearing?' Jean hisses.

'Clothes.'

'Hello, David,' Olive says.

'Aunty Olive.'

Olive bites the inside of her lip to stop the tears welling. He is so young and already his face is stamped with sadness. His lips are full and shaped as any girl's. Fine hair grows above the top one. And he called me Aunty, she thinks.

'Well, you are in a bit of a mess,' Jean says.

'Yep.'

'You used to wear shoes like that to primary school.'

'You wear what you can get around here.'

'Are you all right?' asks Olive.

'Yep.'

'I bought you some chocolates but the man at the door said he'd take them and give them to you later.'

'If they pass inspection.'

'Yes.'

'You haven't any cigarettes, I suppose?' he says.

'Oh no,' Jean says. 'Don't tell me you smoke.'

'There's not much else to do here.'

'I'm disappointed, David. It's a disgusting habit.'

'This is a disgusting place.'

'Whose fault is it you're in here?'

'Mine.'

'Your father would be very upset if he was still alive.'

'He's dead, so he won't be concerned.'

Olive's hand clenches and loosens around the packet of cigarettes in her bag. Her thumb runs on the sharp corners.

'How long have you been smoking?' Jean says.

'I don't know.'

'How many do you smoke a day?'

'Lay off, Mum.'

'Well, I am disappointed. They stain your teeth. There's nothing worse than nicotine-stained teeth.'

Olive places the packet of cigarettes on the table and pushes them over to David.

'Olive!' Jean says.

'Yes?'

'What are you doing with those?'

'I just found them in my bag.'

'Have you got a light?'

Olive rattles the matchbox. David leans forward. She can smell his hair. Striking a match, she holds it until the cigarette is alight.

'That man,' Jean says, nodding to one side. 'That's toilet paper he's got around his head.'

'Yeah, he likes it that way.'

'What's he in for?'

'He nearly killed his wife.'

'Oh my God! Is that her?'

'I suppose so. I don't know.'

The woman unwraps a paper packet and the man takes a sandwich. He looks at it sideways to see the filling then begins eating with great gulping bites.

The child grabs a sandwich but drops it straight away. It separates in the air and lands in two pieces on the floor.

'Butter-side down,' Jean says.

'When will you be out?' Olive asks.

'I don't know.'

'Is there anything you need?'

'Yeah, a cup of tea that doesn't already have sugar in it.'

'I beg your pardon.'

'They make the tea up in an urn and it's already got sugar and milk in it. I would 'ike a plain cup of tea with no sugar and no milk. I would like that very much.'

'Hardly a serious complaint,' Jean says. 'Look at you gulping that cigarette! It's disgusting. They give you cancer, you know.'

'I know.'

'We'll go in a minute,' she says.

'You've only just come.'

'We had to wait for ages and ages. And I have a hair appointment at two.'

'I was down at occupational therapy.'

'Oh my God,' Jean says. 'I don't believe it.'

'What?'

'His toilet paper's slipped!'

'What do you do at occupational therapy?' Olive asks.

'I weave plastic table-mats.'

'Do you enjoy it?'

'No.'

'Look at him.'

'Leave it, Mum.'

'Well just look! I don't believe it.'

The man's paper turban has slipped to the side. Half of his face and one eye is covered and a long loop hangs down at the back. Ignoring it, he continues to bounce the sullen child.

Reaching out tenderly the woman pushes the toilet paper back off his face. She draws on her cigarette.

Jean jiggles her handbag. 'I just don't believe it.' The handbag rattles up and down on the table.

Olive looks at the bare green walls.

'I'll go then,' David says. 'Can I have the smokes?'

'Yes, yes,' Olive says. 'Of course. Take them and...ah, take care and everything.'

'Bye for now,' says Jean, standing briskly.

Olive and Jean wait at the door at one end of the room and David waits at the other. His door opens and he disappears into the crowd of men who push forward to look into the dining room. The door slams and they are gone.

A different man in white trousers locks the door with a key from a ring on his belt. He walks the length of the room.

'Bye, ladies,' he says, stepping aside. He winks and shuts the door behind them and they are back out blinking in the light on the doorstep.

'I made you an appointment at the hairdressers as well,' Jean says.

'For today?'

'This afternoon in the city. I didn't think you'd mind.'

Olive's eye flutters and shuts. 'No,' she says. 'That's fine. Did you see those men in the next room?'

'Olive, your eye.'

'It's nothing. It's stopped now, look. Did you see them?'

'What men?'

'When the door was unlocked for David. There was a group of men just standing there, looking through.'

'I didn't notice.'

'They were all sort of leaning forward, as if they were starving or something.'

'Really, Olive, I don't understand you. Why do you think things like that? Why would they be starving in a hospital? What upsets me is those shoes David had on. Catholic schoolboy's shoes. I don't know how he could wear them. He had a pair like that when he was five. They could be the same ones except they're bigger.'

Olive drives back through the hospital grounds. A long queue of cars has banked up along the road, blocking the hospital exit. Some time passes before they are able to pull out into the traffic.

The hairdressing salon is painted green and red and decorated with bamboo furniture and shiny plants.

'If you'd just sit over there,' the receptionist says.

Olive takes a seat beside a potted palm. It reaches almost to the ceiling before it umbrellas out. The fronds cast a shadow of spiky lines on the walls and floor.

Ah. She is distracted by the tree. What will happen when it reaches the roof? The thought makes her feel claustrophobic, as if a ceiling presses down above her own head. She shifts uneasily in her seat.

Jean is flicking through a magazine. She turns the open pages to Olive. 'Look, that's nice,' she says. 'Get them to do your hair like that.'

'Yes.'

'Or what about this? You could do it with your sort of hair.'

'But my hair is straight.'

'Have a body perm. Ask for a body perm.'

'Yes.'

'Look at those shoes. Aren't they beautiful?'

'They're lovely.'

Jean slaps a magazine on Olive's knee. 'If you don't say what you want they just do anything.'

The models are young and as polished as the paper they are printed on. Olive turns the pages and looks at their faces. She imagines them all to be happy.

'Over here please.' A young woman shows Olive to a chair. Her own hair is bright red and teased up into a messy pile and her fingernails are long blue points.

Olive watches her in the mirror. She ties a bib at the back. Pushing her fingers across Olive's scalp she looks up so their eyes meet.

'What would you like?' she says.

Her blue fingernails appear like spears from the dark hair on Olive's forehead.

'Ah, I'm not exactly sure.'

'It could do with some body.'

'Yes, some body would be nice.'
'And I presume you want it cut.'
'Yes, cut a bit please.' Olive smiles apologetically.
The woman looks evenly in the mirror. 'What sort of conditioner do you use?'
'Ah . . . conditioner. I use egg.'
'Egg?'
'Yes, egg.'
The woman pulls Olive's hair down around her face then lifts it back and drops it. Taking a comb from a tray she runs it through. The dark strands are lifeless.
'Over here. We'll wash it first.'
Olive shuts her eyes while the warm jet of water plays on her scalp. The shampoo is cold. Brisk fingers rub it in, then her hair is rinsed and towelled dry.
Olive returns to the chair. This time she avoids her reflection in the mirror. She watches the green wall where the lines of palm-shadow shiver.
Scissors cut around her ears with a series of snapping sounds. The mirror pulls her eyes back down.
Is that person me? Cheek-bones are sharp angles on either side and her eyes are intense and black. Relax, she thinks. The dark eyes stare. Even as she watches, one flickers half shut.
A middle-aged woman having her hair done. Is that who I am? Something doesn't make sense.
Clumps of hair slide down her shoulders and disintegrate on the floor.
'I don't know what to do,' the face in the mirror says. The black eyes flicker and stare. Keep them open. Muscles in her lids spasm out of control. The young woman doesn't appear to notice.
What don't I want to see? Any of this. Olive looks at the palm-tree shadows.
When she turns back to the mirror her hair is short and shaped around her face but the confusion in her eyes is unchanged. I don't know what to do.
Her neck itches and she wants to cry. She smiles. 'It's lovely,' she says.
'It still needs body.'

'Yes.'

The blue fingernails duck in and out of her hair, rubbing in some thick liquid, then the hairdresser goes over her head with a blow-dryer. She combs it into a stiff puff then sprays it.

Olive climbs down from the chair. She pays at the reception desk.

Jean is still beneath the dryer. She waves her hand.

'I'll meet you back here,' Olive says.

'I can't hear you,' Jean says, too loudly. 'Your hair looks wonderful. Wait till Jim sees.'

'Yes. I'll meet you back here.'

'I'll be another half an hour.'

'Thirty minutes, then.'

Olive steps out into the tide of people on the footpath. A cold wind blows on the nape of her neck. Stopping to one side she lights a cigarette and the match glows a warm colour then flutters out. She sets off walking.

Near the bottom of Queen Street a tall man in a tailored suit and narrow shoes passes on the right. Jim hurries past.

Olive drops the cigarette and grinds it with her heel. 'Jim,' she says.

Unaware, he continues. She hurries behind but he keeps several paces ahead. The straight line of his shoulders moves up and down as he strides along. People cross in front of her.

'Jim.'

Again he doesn't hear.

He stops at the lights and Olive moves forward until she is standing right behind. Near his collar a piece of cotton is a pale line on the charcoal wool of his jacket. She touches it with one gentle finger and it flies off. Still he doesn't look around.

The fabric weave of his suit is tight and fine. Olive looks at the detail. She studies the wefts and the warps.

This man is my husband, she thinks. She can smell his cologne. It's as if he is a total stranger. Has he ever touched me? Have we ever made love?

She speaks right into his ear. 'I'm cold,' she says. 'Jim,

it's me, and I'm cold.'

He continues staring straight ahead.

Olive steps back and her cheeks sting with embarrassment. The words seem to hang in the air. A girl in school uniform catches her eye and looks away.

The crossing lights buzz and Jim steps onto the street. Olive watches from the kerb as people merge and pass over the intersection. His shoulders disappear into the crowd then he is gone.

Olive touches the back of her neck. The skin is textured with cold. Her hair feels like a hat.

Jean takes a dress from Olive's wardrobe and lies it on the bed. 'This one,' she says.

'It's not a very warm dress.'

'I know, but it looks nice.'

'I'm cold though. It's a cold evening.'

'But it's not as if you're going out or anything. Surprise him, Olive. Hurry, he'll be home soon. Your hair looks so nice.' She places the Spanish shoes on the carpet beside the bed.

One toe points out at an angle on the floor as if they too have a posture of their own to impose. Olive pushes her feet into them.

The dress is loose around the middle.

'You need a belt. Borrow my gold one.'

She wraps it around Olive's waist and secures the buckle.

'Earrings now, I think.' She clips two gold hoops onto Olive's ears. They tap against her jaw and pull on her lobes.

Ah, to fling them from the roof of the house, she thinks. She can easily imagine gold spots flying over the rooftops. Her fists clench. 'They look lovely.'

Jean fusses around plucking at the dress and smoothing the fabric out. 'You look marvellous,' she says. 'Look in the mirror. Jim won't recognise you.'

A door opens somewhere at the back of the house. Olive turns her head to listen.

'Hello, hello?' Jim calls.

'In the bedroom,' cries Jean.

'Well, well, well,' he says appearing in the doorway. 'What have we here?'

'Give me your briefcase,' Jean says. 'That's right. What do you think?'

'You've had your hair done as well,' he says. 'You look terrific.'

'Ah.'

'I am impressed. You look really nice. We should all go out for dinner.'

'Oh lovely, lovely.' Jean claps her hands together. There are two noises. One is the softness of palms meeting and the other is the metallic sound of rings clicking together.

Jean and Jim go into the lounge and Olive wanders in behind them.

Jim has three glasses out. He pours an equal measure of gin into each one and tops them with soda. 'It's a celebration,' he says. 'Turn around.'

Olive turns slowly on her high heels and the skirt flies out in an apricot cloud.

'Those earrings look good.'

'I thought you'd forgotten how to do it,' Jim says.

'But she's far too thin.'

'So I see.'

'Look at her legs.'

'I know.'

'Her clothes don't fit, you know. Not really.'

'Still,' Jim says. 'Things are looking up.'

Stop it, Olive thinks. The thought is one long cry.

She turns and there are the lilies. They stand out on the wall. Olive follows the line of the bud as it furls with her eyes. The contours are elegant.

Arum lilies. Four of them on his grave. One for each member of the family, all dead now but for her. And her belly bulging with his first unborn grandchild.

Lilies naked on the soil. The long throats are white in sunlight. The colour is pure.

Olive's fists collapse. Her anger dissolves and runs away while the old sadness swells.

Biting the inside of her cheek she smiles. She lifts her glass. 'Cheers,' she says.

CHAPTER ELEVEN

OLIVE QUEUES FOR coffee at the airport cafeteria. She puts cakes on one plate and sandwiches on another. The china is thick and white and rimmed with a line of maroon.

Jim and Jean whisper in conversation on the far side of the room. Jim's head nods up and down in agreement.

Olive rearranges sandwiches on the plate. She takes the top layer off and turns them around and puts them back again.

The checkout girl pours three cups of coffee and tosses sugar sachets onto the tray.

'Thank you,' Olive says.

As she approaches the table Jim and Jean move their chairs apart. They stare nonchalantly out the windows.

Olive sets the tray down and Jean looks up, smiling brightly.

'Coffee, lovely,' she says.

'Have something to eat.'

'Twenty minutes and I'll be off.'

'I hope you have a good flight.'

'The weather's nice enough, I must say. For winter, anyway.'

'Not much wind today.'

'It's cold though.'

'Yes, it's nippy.'

'Back to Wellington, then.'

'I'll visit David again soon,' Olive says. 'We'll keep an eye on him.'

'He's a silly boy. It will do him good, he has to learn.'

'He's very young.'

'Yes, Olive, I know. But so are your twins, and look

at them.'

Jim smiles and takes a piece of apple shortcake. 'Good girls, the twins,' he says.

'You have another daughter, remember,' says Olive.

'Annette. She never writes.'

'You'll be grandparents soon. Promise you'll ring me when the baby's born?'

'Even at two in the morning?'

'Yes indeed. I'll be dying to hear. Do you hope for a boy or a girl?'

Olive bites into a ham sandwich. 'I don't know.'

'A boy,' Jim says.

Sparrows fly between rafters in the ceiling. One descends onto a neighbouring table and picks at the crumbs there. A cup clatters and the bird flies up in a diagonal line back to the ceiling.

'Olive, I forgot to mention this.'

Olive watches the sparrows flying across.

'Olive.'

'I'm sorry. What's that?'

Jean presses a small box forward then draws it back. Lifting the top, she slides out a glass jar. The squat container is sealed with a blue plastic lid.

'Blemish cream,' says Olive, reading the label.

'For your hand.'

'For what?'

'For that blemish on your hand. The chemist said it was very good.'

'Oh.'

'It will mask it. It's a very unattractive mark.'

'I sort of feel a bit used to it now.'

'You'll feel better with it covered.'

The sparrow comes down to land on the table again and is joined by two others. All three keep nervous watch while they eat.

Unscrewing the blue plastic lid, Olive lifts the jar to her nose. The scent is vague like soap and the cream is thick and tinted beige. 'Thank you,' she says.

Jean's flight is called. 'Come on,' she stands up. 'Is my lipstick all right?'

'Yes, it's fine.'

They walk down the stairs and across to the other side of the airport. People stand in groups or on their own. A child cries.

Jean kisses Jim at the departure gate. She whispers something into his ear. When he turns, the red lipstick lips are printed on his face.

Stepping forward, she hugs Olive. 'Go to the doctor,' she says. 'Sometime soon. Promise me you will.'

'Yes, all right.'

The back of Jean's dress is a blaze of blue, then she is gone.

Olive is alone in the house. The attic room is dusty with neglect. Too much time has passed. She wipes the table and smooths a large sheet of paper.

Lighting a cigarette, she stands at the window and looks out. It is neither the rooftops nor a tumbling winter sky she sees but something else. The inner pictures are more vibrant.

She is aware of the towering hills of a dream. The atmosphere is moody and violent but not devoid of beauty.

Other pictures follow. Sharp bird marks show in naked sand. Each one is a starburst and her own footprints meander amongst them. The shapes are different but balanced.

And then there is the blackbird, given back its life. It soars in a vivid sky.

Stubbing the cigarette out, Olive sets to work. She mixes grey paint for the outline. Her brush moves across the paper in bold strokes. A hill landscape appears.

Crude slabs of land rise steeply and then plunge. Olive squeezes a variety of paints out onto the tin plate. She applies them at random. The colours mix on the paper. Raw umber and Naples yellow deepen with mauve and blue. The hills slowly fill and take on shape.

The sky is indigo. Olive mixes the colour and brushes it roughly at an angle on the paper. In some places the blue deepens to black. The air is dark and moved by some great wind.

There is something wrong with the painting. The yellow highlights are too bright. She dulls the colour down with blue. The light is eerie and cold.

Olive looks at the painting for a moment then puts it aside. Without pausing for a rest, she begins preparations for another.

New hills start as lines dividing the paper. She paints them in rapidly, making the colours intense in the foreground and dull into the distance. A swirling fog moves down from the high country.

Again the sky is dark and strange. A night sky rolls across. Lighten it. Make it day.

But the mood shows through regardless. No amount of paint will change the feeling of night.

Olive props both of the paintings against the wall and stands back.

A savage moonless sky coils above raw hills in both of them. The land folds and swells like parts of a body, but the comparison does nothing to soften the effect.

Sitting on the floor she studies the pictures. What gives them the feeling? Is there too much blue, or is it too dark? Is it something in the shapes themselves?

Her chest sinks. A coldness settles in the room and Olive rolls onto her side on the floor. She curls her body to keep warm.

Half awake and half in a dream, she feels the hours pass. There is no sound to intrude and little sensation.

Olive finds herself on board a boat. Although still in the room, she is on the deck of a boat. Built of wide planks, the vessel seems solid enough and the smell of tar and salt is not unpleasant. It tosses in a truculent sea.

Where is it going? Who is in charge? The land shrinks further and further into the distance and the swell becomes the massive slow swell of deep water.

Olive is uneasy and then afraid. There is no one else on board. Where am I going?

Night approaches and the wake of the boat glows green with phosphorescence. The swell is higher now and some waves tower and break. Their crests trail the same green glow in the dark. There is beauty in the sight but it is soured by fear.

A turbulent sky rolls overhead. A sudden blaze of moonlight shows through, then new black clouds skim over the space.

Cold on the deck, Olive is passive but afraid. The whole thing is out of her control. Lying down, she rolls over, feeling wood hard below.

The sensation takes her back. She lies on the attic floor. The boards are quite without movement beneath her.

Olive pulls herself up into a sitting position. Her fingers are white at the ends. She flexes them slowly. The two paintings are there in front of her.

The night sky in both of them is familiar as the same one in the dream.

How did I get on the boat? She racks her memory but it seems there was no getting on board. She was simply there. 'A passenger,' she mutters.

Angrily, she takes the two paintings and lies them face down on the floor.

She wanders around the house on her way to the bathroom. Once there, she stands looking into the mirror. Her lips are thin and mauve. The dark eyes stare.

Jim will be home soon. Taking a comb, she pushes her hair about, piling it first on one side then the other. She irritates it into a puff with the teeth of the comb then stiffens the whole thing with hairspray.

She rattles about in the cupboard looking for a lipstick tube. Pink covers the cold colour of her lips.

In the bedroom she shakes off her loose trousers and changes into the cream blouse and skirt. Jim's key turns in the lock as she buttons the jacket.

'You've had a good day,' he says. 'I can tell.'

Ahh, she thinks, and her eyelid starts twitching. 'I've had a lovely day, thank you.'

'Doing what?'

'Ah . . . visiting friends and things.'

'You've been out, good. It makes the world of difference.'

'Yes.'

'See Dorothy?'

'Not today. I might call on her tomorrow.'

'Good.'
'How was your day?'
'Very good.'
'Lovely,' Olive says.
'You must make an effort to get out. You look so much better.'
Olive looks at Jim. How can you think it? Two bleak paintings and a dream on the floor. The feeling of deep water and a savage sky. I am so unhappy.
On his way into the lounge Jim reaches out and squeezes her arm. There is little flesh below the elbow. She wanders into the bathroom.
Has he ever touched me? Did we ever make love? Locking the door, she cries silently until there is nothing left.
She splashes cold water onto her face and rubs it dry. When the colour subsides she repairs her make-up.
Pushing the door open, she limps into the kitchen. A casserole thaws in the oven. Lifting the lid, she pokes the icy meat.
'Come and look at this,' Jim calls from the other room.
'Look at what?'
'There's a documentary on cancer.'
'What?'
'Cancer.'
'I can't, I'm getting dinner.'
'This woman they're interviewing now,' he shouts. 'She died three days after filming.'
'Oh, poor woman.'
'Cancer of the bowel, etcetera.'
'I have to cover the salad with gladwrap. There's a cake in the fridge and if I don't cover it it will taste of garlic. The icing will be garlic.'
'Are you coming?'
'I can't. There's gladwrap stuck all around my fingers. It clings like anything.'
'Well hurry. It'll be over soon.'
'Yes.'
'It's about cancer.'
'Jesus, I heard!' Olive leans against the fridge. Her

burning forehead presses on cool white. It will be over soon.

The boat of her dream and the hills and the sky come before her. Voyage into a strange land.

Some part of me will die, she thinks, and the thought is solid as stone. It is too heavy to move aside. A death of sorts approaches.

Olive spends the next morning in the attic room. She sets fresh paints out and a clean piece of paper.

Taking a pencil, she draws the blackbird in flight. Thick pigments fill in each feather.

With a fine brush she spots white on its round eye and the bird comes to life. It hovers ever-watchful on an unmarked plane of white.

She mixes blues for the sky but the shades are too bright. With added yellow they turn into a series of greens. The colours are rich and pleasing.

Using a large brush she spreads the paint thickly so it swirls about.

Outside, a watery sun rises high above the rooftops. A thin light enters the window.

It is not until Olive drops the brushes and stands back that she is able to see what has grown on the paper.

The green bears little resemblance to sky. Rather than support the bird it drags it down. It floats on a swirling ocean. What has happened here?

Change the green. Make it be sky. Olive slashes blue paint across one corner but straight away drops the brush again. The image will not respond.

The glint on the bird's eye is no longer one of life but rather that of desperation.

'Rise up out of the sea!' she cries. But it can't. Or won't.

Deep green water surges and the blackbird floats with wings spread out on either side. It is utterly without flight.

Shocked by the image, Olive rips it into pieces. Wet paint smears her hands and tears fall, diluting it further.

Wiping her hands on the back of her trousers she lights a cigarette. Green paint stains the filter.

She stands at the window looking out. It is midwinter

now, yet the light is still harsh and bright. Even as she watches, the colours of the roofs and trees flatten and lose their richness. The pale harbour glistens. The scene is unpleasantly bleached as if overexposed.

I can't go on. Olive turns her back. The pain in her legs is intense.

The next day is the same. Olive has already bought prepared food for the evening meal and put it aside. She spends most of the morning indoors.

Again, there is something wrong with the light. The day is overcast, but the light is intense and too white. She wanders from room to room. The southern side of the house is gloomy but the attic room is bright.

She has her mind on a cave. Longing for a cave.

She goes out into the garden and once there seeks the shadowy space beneath the rimu. Parting the trailing leaves with her hands, she steps through. Little light can reach her and the smoke from her cigarette rises slowly between the boughs.

The toadstools have swollen to ripeness now, spreading their musty smell in the air. Clearing a large one away with the toe of her shoe, Olive sits down. She can feel the damp soil through her clothes. Bones are sharp against the ground and her back is against the trunk.

The garden is silent. There is no evidence of people nearby. Never has she felt so cold.

Late in the day she stands stiffly and returns to the house. She washes in the bathroom and cleans her teeth.

Every remnant of energy is required to dress for Jim. Between patting make-up on and fluffing her hair she rests against the bathroom wall. The minutes tick by.

The jar of blemish cover sits on the sill. She unscrews the lid and lifts it to her nose, then dips in one finger and spreads a layer of the skin-coloured cream across the bloodstain on her palm. It settles like mud into the lines on her hand.

As it dries the colour fades. The bloodstain is partially disguised.

Jim uncorks a bottle of white wine to go with the meal. 'Chicken, good,' he says. 'White wine with white meat. Let's celebrate.'

'Celebrate what?'

'Your recovery. Pass me the potato salad. Is it potato salad? We don't usually have it in the winter.'

'Have I been sick?'

'Don't bullshit, Olive. You know what I'm talking about. Mm, this dressing is good. It's not your usual dressing.'

'It's a new recipe.'

'It's an improvement on the old one.'

'Yes.'

'I must say I was worried about you for a moment there.'

'Yes.'

'Still, you're looking good now. It did you the world of good having Jean here. I knew it would get you back on your feet.'

No, no, no, Olive thinks. I hated it. I'm not happy, I'm not happy. I'm dying. It will all be over soon.

'Yes,' she says. 'I'm feeling good.'

'And you're looking it. A bit of make-up suits you. And you're back into cooking decent meals again. This chicken is very tender. Look at this breast. It's just falling apart.'

Olive turns her head towards the kitchen. The door is open and from the corner of her eye she can see the foil-lined bag she had carried the chicken home in. A chicken bought steaming hot from the delicatessen and reheated for dinner. Screwed in a fatty ball, the bag sits on the edge of the bench.

'Pour me another wine, please,' she says.

The blemish cream seems to dull the feeling in her palm. Holding the glass of chilled wine the sensation could be one of cold or it could be heat. It seems impossible to tell.

'It's quite a relief,' Jim says.

'Yes, well everything's just fine now.'

'Excellent, excellent.'

I'm dying, Olive thinks. Some part of me will die. Can't he see that? Can't he tell?

Jim pushes his plate back. 'More chicken would be nice,'

he says.

Olive takes two grey woollen blankets upstairs to the attic room. One drops from her hand to the floor and she pins the other over the window. The room becomes a grotto. Ahh, a cave.

In this half-light the picture of the storm at sea takes on a sullen and brooding aspect.

Picking the two hill paintings up from the floor she turns them over. Something in them is too powerful. She is afraid.

Dropping them again she spreads the blanket and then lies down on it. She lies there for a long time.

Eventually she sits up, then rises to her feet. She switches the light on and blinks until her eyes have adjusted.

There is one piece of paper left. She stares at the blankness of it. The blackbird is dead. Birds are too frail. The hills and skies of her mind are too savage and the forest is too dark.

There is one other image. Olive cries out for the roundness of eggs. Her eyes shut but the picture won't come.

A simple egg. She can't see it.

Squares and triangles appear. Breaking into lines, they fall apart. Black lines and red lines move from the left and back over to the right. Now they are spreading out and a slick emerges from below. A deep rolling sea extends in all directions. No land shows on the horizon.

An egg, she thinks. A smooth white oval. Blue. Speckled. Brown or spotted. There is no hush and there is no egg. She is unable to visualise it.

The cold sea looms. Grey-green waves topple into white at the crests. The troughs are black. It is a deep ocean, or even bottomless.

Olive's eyes snap open and the piece of paper is a blaze of white and the lightbulb is a yellow flare. Downstairs the telephone rings and rings.

Olive switches the light off and lies down on the blanket. She sleeps through another slow, cold day.

Olive clears the breakfast dishes and takes them to the sink. Turning both taps on, she watches the water flow. She washes the plates first and then the cups.

The doorbell rings and she freezes. Her wrists rise up from a froth of detergent. One finger moves in the water. A submerged saucer is a vague blur at the bottom of the sink. She watches that. The doorbell rings again.

Olive draws out her hands and dries them on a tea-towel. The detergent is lemon-scented. Keep quiet, she thinks. Stay still. I should hide.

There is a dark space beneath the table. At first Olive just looks at it, then she is down on the floor and crawling in. She sits with her knees up under her chin and the table-top hard on the back of her head. The wall supports her from behind.

Footsteps sound down the side of the house then on the steps and the knocking starts up at the back door. Feet shuffle on the porch. For a long time the person stands silently.

Olive watches the back door from beneath the table. 'Go away,' she mutters in her throat.

Knuckles rap on the wood again and this time the doorknob turns. The door swings slowly open and Dorothy steps in. Her coat is huge and blue, with square pockets.

She looks straight at Olive and her eyes squint then open wide. 'Olive!' she cries. 'Are you all right?'

'I'm just sitting under the table.'

'Oh, Olly, you're not all right, are you?'

'No.'

'Do you want me to go?'

'No, please don't.'

Dorothy bends from the waist and her moon face peers into the space beneath the table. 'Shall I put the jug on?' she asks.

She bites her lower lip and Olive can only stare at the point where the tips of her front teeth show.

'Shall I make a cup of tea?'

'Yes,' Olive whispers. 'Let's have a nice cup of tea.' She lets one leg stretch forward, then the other.

'That's better.'
'I didn't know it was you. I'm sorry.'
'It's all right. I'll get the jug on, then.'
Dorothy's feet disappear into the kitchen. Water runs in the sink and the kettle lid clicks. After a time her feet reappear in their flat brown shoes.
'Are you going to come out?'
'I don't think I can.'
'Here, let me help you.'
'It's so hard to move. There's something wrong with my legs.'
'Why didn't you call me?'
'I don't know.'
Dorothy's hands reach down and Olive struggles out from the confined space. She straightens her back slowly until she is standing.
'Your hands are ice. Oh, Olly, look at you.'
'Well. I don't know. What about you? Are you all right now?'
'Yes,' Dorothy says. 'Sort of. I've put on more weight, you know. Nothing fits.'
'And I've lost it.'
'Yes, you have. What's wrong?'
'I'm dying.'
Alarm opens Dorothy's eyes. 'You mustn't say things like that.'
'Well, maybe I'm not dying exactly but I feel like something is, or some part of me is.'
'What do you mean?'
'I don't know.'
'Are you unwell?'
'I think I might be.'
'Unwell with what?'
'I don't know. I keep thinking of cancer.'
Colour surges into Dorothy's face and her voice reduces to a whisper. 'Have you been to the doctor?'
'No.'
'Then what makes you think it?'
'It's my body. I can tell. Something is terribly amiss.'
'No, no, you're wrong there, I'm sure. You're depressed,

that's all.'

'I'm wasting away. And I have this pain in my legs.'

'How much weight have you lost?'

'I don't know.'

'Do you eat enough?'

'I don't eat very much.'

'And have you spoken to Jim?'

'No.'

Dorothy reaches for Olive's arm. She squeezes it gently. 'You're depressed,' she says. 'Go to the doctor for a check-up, but I'm sure you'll find that's what it is.'

'I guess you're right.' Olive tries to smile but her lips won't move across her teeth.

The electric kettle whistles in the kitchen. Dorothy goes through to make the tea.

She brings the pot to the table. The cups are blue and the tea when she pours it is amber. Dark tea leaves spin in a clockwise direction.

Dorothy's fingers are white sausages. They barely fit through the handle of her cup. She has taken her wedding band off but the indentation remains. The skin there is smooth and pale.

Olive sips her tea. The liquid is hot and bitter. She looks at the ceiling and tries not to cry.

'I know of something that would really cheer you up,' says Dorothy.

'What's that?'

'The trouble is we'd have to go out to see it.'

'Out?'

'It's not far. It's just something I saw on the way here.'

'Would we walk?'

'Are your legs too sore?'

'I could manage.'

'Good then.' Dorothy buttons her coat.

'What is it?'

'Wait and see. It's something nice, I promise you.'

'I'm cold,' Olive says. 'It's so cold.'

They go out through the front door. Dorothy pulls it shut behind them.

The day is bleak and bright. A concrete-mixer grinds

on the driveway of the house next door. Three spades in a row stick up out of the lawn. There is no one in attendance.

Olive and Dorothy set off down the hill and the sound fades. The street is quiet.

An old man prods in his garden near the bottom. French marigolds grow along the front boundary but the plants have twisted and the blooms are poor. The soil is dry clay between them.

An old man works in his garden. Is he happy? What does he think?

The light is wrong again. The clay is ocherous and without life and the old man's fingers scrape uselessly.

'The place needs painting and tidying up,' Dorothy says. 'So does ours for that matter.'

What is this all about? What can I do? The bloodstain itches and burns on Olive's hand and she stops to rub it on her coat. 'The tide is low,' she says.

'Yes, it is.'

They look out over the harbour. Mud stretches between the shore and the waterline. No birds forage today.

Olive scans the sky. The entire expanse is empty.

'Are you warmer yet?'

'I'm very cold. I don't know why I'm so cold.'

'It's winter.'

'Yes.'

'I'm roasting,' Dorothy pants. 'We go along this street here.'

The properties are larger further along and tall trees lean over the footpath. A Norfolk pine forms a huge symmetrical tower. The branches throw a shadow of jagged lines on the iron roof of a garage. The roof is blue and the lines are navy grey.

Riveted by the zig-zag pattern, Olive stops.

Dorothy waits a few steps ahead. 'What is it?'

'That pattern on the roof.'

'The iron?'

'No, the shadow. It makes me think of something.'

Dorothy's flushed face turns upwards. 'Does it?'

Olive looks back to the roof. What is it? The particular

shade of blue sparks something, but more than that it is the shapes. Jagged lines cut one way and the other.

'Lines like my thoughts,' she says. She imagines the inside of her head as a bowl. It is blue and even as a thrush's egg and her thoughts are jagged lines on the smooth surface. They are too deeply etched.

A high wind moves through the tree and the shadowed lines weave. A picture of my thoughts.

'They're all angles,' she says. 'There's not a curve there.'

'It's not far now.'

There is nothing soft and round. I can't go on.

The wind is a thin high whistle.

Dorothy points along the street. 'Just at the end. Just along there,' she explains.

The path changes to red gravel chips. A brindled dog meanders ahead, sniffing on the grass verge. It lifts a leg on an oleander bush and continues. Its tongue is a pink slice between white teeth.

'You can see the dog's breath,' says Olive. 'That's how cold it is.'

'It's the shade. Wait until it's back in the sun.'

'Yes, I suppose so.'

'Well, here we are.'

Olive glances vaguely around. The houses are old and immaculate. Gardens sweep elegantly across the lawns. What should I be looking at? 'It's nice down here,' she says.

The dog barks and paws at something in a hedge. A grey cat runs off and up into a tree.

'Can you see what I brought you here to see?'

'I'm not sure. What is it?'

'Look over there.'

'What is it?'

'The climbing roses will be out soon, Olive.'

The world spins. 'What?' Olive whispers. For a moment it is as if she is blind.

'Olive, Olly, what's the matter? Here, hold my arm. What's the matter?'

Olive gropes in her head for something to hold. There is nothing there. It is a bowl or cavity scoured with serrated lines. There is nothing else.

'My father said that once,' she says at last.

'Said what? Your hands are all shaking.'

'Where are the roses? I can't see any.'

Dorothy swings her arm around. 'Climbing on that wall there,' she says. 'We're not close enough, that's all.'

'There aren't any.'

'Look up there. They'll be out soon.'

'But they won't be,' Olive wails.

'I noticed the buds on the way up this morning and I thought of you.'

'Buds?'

'Yes, you know.'

Olive walks over to the wall. The rose climbs all over it. Just now the plant supports neither foliage nor buds. Her hand is white amongst the thorns. 'They won't be out soon,' she cries. 'There aren't any buds.'

Tears stream down her face and fall onto her hands. Her legs bend and she is sitting on the gravel.

Dorothy rushes over to the plant. She turns back and her face is crimson. 'Oh,' she says.

'They won't be out soon,' Olive sobs.

'Let me help you up.'

'I can't.' Olive's legs stick out straight ahead like a child's. Gravel chips cling to her stockings.

'Olly.' Dorothy wrings her hands. 'I was sure I saw buds. I must have imagined it. They were the apricot ones that open out cream. I'm so sorry. You're very upset. You can't sit there on the footpath.'

'I can't, I can't.'

A great desolation presses down. It is a cold wind from above and welling up from below. The tears won't stop. It feels like the end.

After a time a car passes and stops. It reverses alongside and the door opens. A man gets out.

Olive is vaguely aware of him standing above her. His legs are bare and he wears running shoes. A gold stripe marks the side of each one.

The light is too harsh. Neither the shoes nor the footpath below them look real, yet every detail stands out clearly.

Each gravel chip is defined.

Dorothy's voice and his are a murmur above her head and now he's bending down. 'I'll give you ladies a lift home,' he says.

Olive nods but cannot move. Her legs will make no response.

Strong hands lift her to her feet and she is guided and half-carried to the car.

'You don't weigh much,' the man says, helping her into the back seat.

Dorothy climbs in alongside.

The motor starts and they pull out onto the street. Olive turns her swollen face and sees again the thick branches of the old climbing rose. Bare branches ramble on the high brick wall.

The climbing roses will be out soon, Olive. 'Ahh,' she cries.

Dorothy holds Olive's hand on her lap and gives the man instructions. 'Halfway up the hill,' she says. 'The white house on the right.'

He swings into the driveway.

The man assists Olive up the steps to the front door. She watches the gold stripes on his shoes.

'I'll be all right now,' she says. 'Thank you.'

Dorothy makes the bed and fills a hotwater bottle. 'What can I do for you?' she says plumping the pillows.

Olive pulls her legs into the bed. Her whole body is numb. 'I'll be fine,' she says. 'I'll sleep.'

Dark jagged lines on a blue iron roof. 'Don't tell Jim. He wouldn't understand.'

'Of course. Is there anything else I can do?'

'No, I'll sleep.'

Dorothy treads sadly up the hall and pulls the front door shut.

Olive hauls herself out of bed and up the stairs to the attic room. The grey blanket covers the window. She sleeps in the dark.

CHAPTER TWELVE

JIM BUTTONS HIS shirt at the breakfast table. 'Now that you're feeling better,' he says, 'it's time to entertain again.'

'People? Have people here?'

'Of course, people. What else? I've invited four guests to dinner on Thursday night.'

'This Thursday?'

'That's the one. Bill and Norman from work and their wives.'

Olive coughs until the tears stream down her face. 'That's fine,' she says.

'Cook something nice, won't you?'

'Yes, of course.'

Jim spreads a layer of blackberry jam on a piece of toast and takes a bite. 'Good. I'll ring the twins and see if they can come.'

'Yes.'

His teeth have made a horseshoe shape in the purple jam. He hurries to finish his breakfast.

'I'm going to work with Bob,' he says. 'Must dash.'

'Goodbye.'

Olive waits for the sound of the front door closing. As soon as Jim has gone she takes herself upstairs to the attic room.

Hooking the blanket, up, she pushes the window open. She lights a cigarette and smokes it leaning against the sill. Smoke drifts out into the morning and away. The light is discordant. The familiar nausea stirs.

Stepping back, she lets the blanket fall. The room is dark again. Sleep calls and curled on the hard floor she submits.

The dream which comes is so vivid as to be real. For the time being she presumes that it is.

She is downstairs in the house. Jim has a number of long strips of green paper. He stands there, holding them out to her.

Olive takes a piece from his hands and can see that one side is coated with wet glue. She tries to paste it to the wall but the paper bubbles and puckers and sticks to her hands. Her fingers move. She is aware of the feeling of glue on her palms.

She studies the already existing wallpaper. Green sprigs scatter across a white background. Gaps show on every seam. The strips are to cover the board and plaster showing through.

Jim is impatient. Pressing another piece of paper to the wall, Olive runs her hands down to smooth it. The colour is ill-matched to the wallpaper behind and the seams are crooked. The next strip of paper falls apart and she has to stick the pieces together. The harder she tries, the worse the walls look. It is a pointless exercise.

Moving to one side, she discovers something sticking out. A handle protrudes from the wall and there is a door. It seems scarcely believable she has never noticed it before.

'Jim!' she cries but he has wandered off.

The door opens to a flight of stone steps. They sweep down and around. The surfaces are old and worn and the air is different.

Olive discovers another level to the house. It has been there unknown all along. The sound in this part of the building is the sound of no noise at all.

Many rooms lead off from a central corridor. Each one is filled with beauty and colour and light. Paintings of indescribable richness line the walls. She wanders awestruck from one to the next.

Somewhere deep in the house she encounters a closed door. The number seventeen is engraved upon it. Recognising it as her own number Olive turns the handle and steps through.

The room is perfectly bare. The walls and the ceiling are white. There is nothing here at all, yet the atmosphere is pregnant. Olive runs her fingers along the smooth wall. They make no mark, neither does any trace of the white come off on her fingertips. She is waiting.

In the next moment the air fills with flashing colour and the birds are in the room. They dip and swoop around and around in every colour of the rainbow. Rose and lemon and blue blaze against the white. Their flight is not inhibited by the confined space. They have never moved so freely or been so bright. It is a sight of unbelievable beauty.

Olive opens her eyes to the grey of the blanket and the dimness of the attic room. Her hand is blue and open on the floor alongside her. As she watches, her fingers move and the hand forms a tight fist around her thumb. Pale freckles show on her knuckles. You have your mother's hands. Who said that? I can't remember. It is too long ago.

Pale drifts of dust mark the floorboards. Olive looks at her hand lying blue on the dusty wood. The moment is critical. Something taps at the window. The noise stops as abruptly as it started. The blue hand doesn't move.

After a time the tapping starts up again and increases. Olive rolls onto her back. The room is black all around her. No longer can a decision be avoided. Live or die, she thinks. It is too big. The noise at the window scatters the thought and she is drifting away. Time passes in a dream.

The noise continues, cutting in and fading and then starting up again. It interferes and it irritates. Shutting her eyes, she moves away. When they open again the room is darker still.

Rising to her feet, Olive stumbles against the wall. Her legs are slow and without feeling. The blanket at the window comes away in her hand and light floods in. Blinded, she pushes the window open and is almost knocked off her feet by the birds. The whole room is filled with them.

Olive turns from one direction to the other. Her mouth is open with astonishment. These birds glow in every colour against the white. Circling around, their wings brush her face and lift her hair. The sound of their flight is the sound of a hush.

There can be no further happiness. Birds strong and bright, she thinks, but even as she thinks it the energy seems less. Too late Olive realises they are leaving. The birds stream out through the window as suddenly as they came.

Once above the rooftops they assume a tight formation. Leaning out through the window, Olive watches their departure. Now they are flying straight against the blue line of ranges to the west. They quickly diminish to small spots of colour and then they are gone.

Olive pulls the window closed. There is no longer a decision to be made.

Olive brushes her hair at the bedroom mirror. 'My face is white.'

'It always is,' Jim says.

'Am I always this pale?'

'You are.'

'I had a dream.'

Jim folds the blankets back and climbs into bed. His pyjamas are in blue and white stripes and the sheets are crisp cotton. 'Summer sheets,' he says, frowning.

'I'll change them tomorrow.'

'They're too cold for winter.'

'I'm sorry.'

'Where are the flannelette ones?'

'I had a dream.'

Jim snaps the bedside lamp on. 'Did you?'

'I dreamt there was another level to the house.'

'Another floor?'

'Sort of. Downstairs. But it wasn't underground, exactly, because there were windows. I don't think I looked through them. I'm not sure.'

'I see.' Taking the evening paper Jim spreads it on the bed.

'There were lots of rooms. All sorts of rooms.'

'Mm.'

'And there were libraries and art galleries.'

'There's an article here about psychiatric hospitals.'
'Why did you say that?'
'Because there is. Look.'
'Jim, it's important.'
'What is?'
'The dream.'
'You do know what dreams are?'
'It was a lovely dream.'
'Dreams are mental garbage. The junk you accumulate during the day. The throwaways.' Jim nods his head as if speaking to a child. 'This dream interpretation business of yours is nonsense. You're always going on about dreams.'
'You and I were squatting in a drab little corner of this big house and I was trying to fix it up so it would be okay, but I couldn't. I couldn't do it. And you see, we didn't even know that all these other rooms were there.'
Jim turns another page of the newspaper and scans the headlines. 'Very interesting,' he says.
'I was trying to patch the walls up with pieces of green paper but it wasn't working. And then I found these other rooms and they were like art galleries.'
'I see.'
'That's what it's like!' Olive cries. 'It feels like that. I can't stay here any longer.'
'Look,' says Jim, slapping the newspaper. 'Let's not start up with this crap again.'
Olive's face is tight with anger in the mirror. Jim rises up in the bed behind her and the newspaper slides to the floor.
'This here is reality!' he roars. His hands chop to emphasise the words. 'This here right now. The rest is bullshit and I won't have you indulging in it. You're ruining our marriage.'
Olive's hand shoots out from her side and before she knows it has swept across the dressing-table top. Make-up and trinkets and the big blue vase fly into the air. Fragments of china explode about the room. Olive stares at her hand in disbelief. Beads of blood well up in a lopsided line along her knuckles and a sliver of bone glints blue-

white and slick.

Jim leaps from the bed in slow motion. His eyes are slits so no colour shows. He stops and his arms are up as if to strike. Blood spreads and drips from Olive's hand to her nightdress. She watches the spreading stain.

'Christ almighty!' Jim says and his voice is low and dangerous. 'I don't believe it.'

'I didn't mean to do it.' Seeing his face, Olive shuts her eyes.

'You didn't mean to do it? I saw you do it! How can you say you didn't mean to do it? It was a wedding present. You know how valuable it was, Olive. Christ almighty!' His arms drop to his sides and swing.

Spinning around, she steps out through the bedroom door. The lounge is dark. Even so, the white shapes which are the painted arum lilies show up on the wall. Olive punches the light switch and they leap out at her. Two lilies stand tall and the furled bud leans to one side. At the sight of them the anger drains from her body and the old sadness swells.

Humble lilies on his grave, she thinks. Pure white and marble-smooth against fresh earth. And lilies on the farm. A little girl in an old brown coat wanders through. She will stop to pick lilies but all the while there is the baby to be fed and the clothes to wash. Little overalls dry in a row on the hedge.

Mummy's gone away and father is so sad. Look at him staring out through the window.

Collapsing onto the floor, Olive cries and cries. Nothing can stop it. The pain is too big. Immobilised, she cries out loud and even when the tears stop the sobbing continues. It is a strange, primitive noise, rising from the very depths.

Jim leaves for work without having spoken a word.

Olive takes an old suitcase and begins to pack. She folds three pairs of trousers and a thick coat. The cream suit is ghostly in a drycleaner's plastic bag. It hangs in the front of the wardrobe. She leaves it and the rack of dresses behind.

A small triangle of china shows on the carpet near the bedroom door. Picking it up, she turns it in her fingers. The outside is glossy blue and the inside is matt white. The other pieces have been cleared away. Dropping it into her pocket, Olive feels the sharp edge through the fabric on her thigh. It rubs all the way up to the attic room.

This part of the house has never been so still. The blanket is crumpled in folds beneath the window where it fell and the light coming in is cold and grey. On the sill the bird marks barely show.

Olive folds one of the blankets and packs it with the boxes of paints and brushes. Taking the flying picture from the wall she places it on top of the case and shuts the lid. Downstairs the telephone rings and rings.

Olive stands staring and the dream starts up again. Nothing moves. Time passes in this way. Who can tell how much time? A lone seagull glides past the window. Its head turns from side to side and the bird's wings are frozen for the updraught. Olive watches it pass and then she is back in the room.

Taking the hibiscus painting from the table she rips it into pieces. They fly from her hands. Scraps of red and green and white swirl about before coming down to settle in the dust on the floor.

'Goodbye,' she says and her words are strange in the quiet.

Her shoes clatter on the stairs as she descends.

Spreading a clean sheet of paper on the kitchen table she stands there looking at it. It would be easy to be seduced by the blankness.

'I have to go,' she writes, and the pen twists and turns in her hand. A bird appears soaring in flight on the page.

Olive walks out through the front door. She puts the suitcase in the car then goes down the side path to the back garden.

'Goodbye garden,' she says.

The orchard is a barren mass of branches and trunks and the flowerbeds are bare turned earth. The spring bulbs have not come through. She scans the bottom boundary. No pale new growth flickers. Turning her back, she returns to the car. The motor starts easily. She backs out of the driveway but the crying has begun.

Letting the car coast down the hill she rubs her eyes with one hand. She steers around the corner at the bottom of the street while barely seeing at all. She drives slowly through the neighbourhood. Her jacket front is wet with tears.

Once on the open road they have finished. Following the harbour she drives to the west. There are few cars on the motorway. The tide is full and blue and banks of shells are white. Mangroves stand up out of the water and sea birds pick along the shore. Olive winds the window down and wind whips into the car, lifting her hair and bringing new water to her eyes. The air is cold and clean with salt.

The battered suitcase sits like a passenger on the front seat beside her. A scar runs diagonally across the lid. Looking at it, she laughs.

Olive pulls up and parks outside a suburban dairy. She peers through the window then enters to buy food for the journey. She stacks bread and oranges and chocolate on the counter.

A woman in a blue smock bounces a fat baby on her hip. He smiles and two teeth are pearly squares above his bottom lip.

'A packet of Benson and Hedges, please,' Olive says.

They slide across the counter and the baby reaches out with both arms.

'That's a nasty cut on your hand,' the woman says. 'You should dress it.'

'It looks worse than it is.'

'Shouldn't it be stitched?'

'Thank you, but it's fine.'

She is driving again. Before long the road begins to climb into the foothills of the Waitakere Ranges and houses give way to orchards. Old apple trees huddle together, twisted with age and cold. White flowers break into bloom at their roots.

Pulling onto the shoulder of the road, Olive parks the

car. She gets out and takes a few steps to one side. The land slopes down into a valley and at the bottom a row of poplars separates the orchard from bush. Grass has been left to grow between the trees. The white bloom spreads right down. Onion flowers, she thinks, but they are snowdrops.

'Snowdrops!' Olive cries.

Rising above the grass, the bell-shaped flowers nod. The delicate movements possess the first flavour of spring.

She bounces back into the car. Further along the road the orchards end and bush covers the land.

Olive lights a cigarette and drives with one hand. Where am I going? What will I do? It seems of no concern.

As the road climbs higher it twists into a series of corners. Ferns and bushes crowd in on either side and tall trees reach over above. Less light can penetrate. The weeping foliage of an occasional rimu stands out a shade yellower than the rest.

'Rain trees,' she says and then it is raining.

Fine banks of mist sweep across the bush and the green is muted. Olive changes down a gear and the car slows. Winding the window down she throws her cigarette out. The smells of earth and rain flood in.

A red truck appears ahead. It approaches slowly and Olive has a fleeting glimpse of a figure crouched forward over the wheel. Windscreen wipers slash from side to side and jets of muddy water spray out from the tyres as the truck passes.

The road is deserted as before. The rain eases to mist. Something flashes ahead and Olive's foot jumps to the brake. The visibility is poor but the road seems clear now. Her foot moves back to the accelerator but the flash occurs again and again she is braking. A sudden point of light bursts against a dripping backdrop of bush.

Pulling over to the side of the road she stops and steps out of the car. There is nothing out of the ordinary. The silence makes her nervous. She pulls her jacket tight around her shoulders.

A silver swallow appears from the mist. Even in this dim light the plumage is luminous. Swooping down, the small bird circles the car and flies back into the haze.

A great breath fills Olive's lungs. She takes her raincoat from the back of the car and fills the pockets with chocolate and oranges. Pushing her arms into the sleeves she locks the car doors then sets off walking along the road in the direction of the bird's disappearance.

The road is loose metal and potholed with puddles of brown water. Her shoes crunching on stones make the only sound. Heavy boughs reach across and disappear into the fog. Something flashes to the right and she turns but it has already gone.

A great kauri grows at this point. The trunk is mottled and solid as rock. It rises straight up to the level of the mist without branching. Above that, the tree is obscured. With a flare of silver the bird darts out from behind the trunk. Swooping low over the road, it turns and flies back to the kauri. Olive waits but the swallow is hidden from sight again.

Crossing to the tree, she places her palm flat against the bark. Double lines of white resin have run and hardened on either side. She can feel the life murmur deep inside the wood. The vegetation beside the tree on one side thins to a gap. Olive squeezes past the trunk as wet leaves press in on her then open out to form a path. The kauri rises up behind her.

Silver flashes once and then again. The bird flits ahead and waits. Damp bush reaches down on all sides and every branch Olive touches sheds a load of raindrops. Her hair is plastered wet on her forehead.

The light is poor but the path is clear. In time, the bird ahead is joined by several others. They twist and turn, fishbelly bright.

Rounding a corner, Olive stops. The bush opens out into a clearing. The rain has ceased. A great forested hill rises up on one side and at its base a creek flows down into a pool. Water gurgles on its way past mossy boulders. Stepping down onto the bank, Olive follows its course to the pool. Again a great breath fills her body. The water is still and deep and black. Irresistibly, she is drawn to it.

Closer and closer she moves until her feet are on a shelf

of grey rock at the very edge. Nothing shows through the water.

She peers into the dark for a shape or shadow but there is nothing. No weed grows or floats on the surface. The pool is deep and still except for a quiet swirl which marks the point where fresh water flows in. The corresponding overflow is even more subtle. The water drains off silently. No visible current moves across the middle of the pool.

Olive sits down on the flat rock to watch. Drawing up her knees she clasps her arms around them. A dragonfly hovers over the water and its reflection is sharp below. It glides off and out of sight.

Olive looks up briefly. The birds are nowhere to be seen. She sits staring into the water. Time passes and the pool is all she is aware of. Deep, deep water. Nothing else exists.

Nightfall approaches and shadows move down from the bush. The pool is black as before but less glossy now. Olive drags her eyes away. Taking an orange from her raincoat pocket she peels it and splits the fruit into segments. She sucks the sweet wet flesh until it has finished. Throwing the pieces of peel out into the water near the lower end of the pool she watches the pale shapes float then turn lazily as the draining current carries them off.

She tosses a small pebble and slow ripples radiate out from the splash. After a time they die away and the pool is blank as before. It is a sheet of black glass and now the far bank is also dark. Bush and sky merge for the night.

A yellow ball appears at some stage. It is the moon. It ascends full and bright over the skyline. The bush murmurs with nocturnal noises. A morepork cries. Cloud strands pass over the moon, splitting the globe into halves. The edges of moving mist glow gold on grey. The reflection in the pool is also divided by cloud but when it sweeps away the ball is intact. On water the gold moon is dull. The pool is black.

Olive lies down on the shelf of rock. Her feet extend over the edge and her face presses against the cold. Regardless of the discomfort, sleep comes easily. It brings nothing on this night. No awareness or images intrude.

She awakens suddenly. It is still dark and her body is pained with cold. Needles jab at her temples and her eyes ache with the slightest movement. Rolling onto her back, she squints at the sky. The moon has moved over but stars still shine. The pool is vacant as before. The morepork sounds and something crashes in the undergrowth. Soon she is asleep again. She stays that way until dawn.

The sky is lighter now and the stars have gone. A watery sun silently rises. Olive pulls herself onto her knees. Her palms are flat on the rock. She holds the posture for some time then stands unsteadily. Pain knaws in her legs. Her bones are on fire. I can't go on.

She moves slowly, one foot pushing in front of the other. Turning away from the pool she limps up into the clearing behind, stumbling around its edge.

On the far side a track leads up into the bush-covered slope but Olive passes this by and returns to the pool.

She is back on the rock shelf and sitting down. With numb fingers she takes a block of chocolate from her pocket and tears the wrapper back. Placing a piece on her tongue she sucks at the sweetness.

The early light is pale and blue but the water is black as before. Olive sits and looks. Her legs stretch out and ache on the rock. The sun rises and the blue takes on a warmer tone but the pool remains black. I can't go on.

Leaning forward, she dips her fingers into the water and it is icy. In time the cold stops and she is able to lower her hand further.

A disturbance cuts the air somewhere behind. Silver explodes all around her and the birds are in the air over the pool. The brightness from above blazes on the water's surface. Forming a tighter band, they fly back over the clearing. Olive follows them with her eyes. Their movements are fluent and graceful, but urgent too. Through all this the water beckons. She lies down on her stomach and as her hands sink lower the water rises up her raincoat sleeves.

The birds swoop and duck low. Without even looking,

Olive is aware of them. Their flight agitates the air. She withdraws her hands and they are pink and without feeling. The bloodstain is darker than ever. She swings around so it is her feet which enter the water. It runs freezing into her shoes and socks and creeps up her legs. She can feel the wet fabric of her trousers.

She is submerged now to the thighs. Half in the water, she balances her stomach against the rock edge. Sink in, sink down. One small movement is all it would take. The water calls and its voice is strong.

Olive hovers on the edge. Her face rests on cool rock. It smells of earth and lichen. Her mind is a blank. The water calls. A fly buzzes past. The smell of moss rises. A burst of movement drags her eyes up. The birds circle on the side of the hill. Darting between the treetops they fling themselves up into clean air.

A battle rages, but Olive is without thought. It is too difficult. She balances and the water is black. So sweet.

The birds rise in a flash. She can see them from the corner of her eye. She looks instead to where her hands grip fractures in the rock. Freckles show on her knuckles. A dark scab has formed over the cut. It makes an angry slash. The surrounding skin is blue. These hands, she thinks.

Beside her left wrist a seedling grows from a flaw in the rock. There are three full leaves and a curled bud. Lines run out from a central vein on each leaf. The thrusting tip is green. A perfect plant grows from a fracture in the solid rock.

The birds whirl by. Swooping up, they turn and spiral down. Their breeze gives movement to the plant. The gentle leaves sigh. Olive shuts her eyes.

'It is a choice.' The voice is rough and anguished and sounds inside her head. It is her own voice. The egg is there, spinning in space. The shell is bluish and speckled. Half-shadowed, it turns slowly against a backdrop of black. An egg. The perfect egg. Ahh.

Olive's hands grip the rock and her legs swing out, shedding water from the pool. Rolling over, she lies face down and her eyes are shut again. The egg spins. The oval shape is full and immaculate.

'To die without thinking,' she mutters.

Pulling herself up she rises stiffly to her feet. Water trickles down her legs, darkening the rock.

The pool calls and its voice is dark honey. Olive presses her hands to her ears. She is stumbling. Her legs won't work. She falls down onto her knees and crawls away.

The birds have come down now. They hop in a tight band on the hillside path and stand there waiting. Seventeen birds, she thinks, without having counted them. Sixteen silver and one of emerald green. She can see the bright lime colour amongst the rest. The bird that is me. But there is no energy. I can't go on.

She lies down on the edge of the clearing. What can I do? Her face presses into the grass but there is something else now. The smell of pennyroyal fills the air. Lifting her head, she breathes it in. Low plants grow amongst spears of grass and as she sets off moving on her hands and knees they flatten and the fragrance is released.

The smell of pennyroyal. Lavender flowers and sunny days. Ahh. I must move on. So little strength.

The birds start up. They dance across her vision and she is rising to her feet to follow. Their flight is slow and they dart back and forwards at eye level on the path ahead.

Her first steps are halting but she is on the track. Bush presses in on either side and the taller trees meet together above her. Long roots wind across the ground. She staggers, placing one lifeless foot in front of the other. As she moves her legs regain feeling and when she looks back the pool is no longer in sight.

'Go back,' she mutters but the words are hollow. The birds float on the air ahead and there will be no going back now.

I *can* go on. The pain in her legs decreases.

'I *can* go on, I *can* go on.' She says it over and over and the pain ceases and walking becomes easy.

The path climbs uphill at a steady angle and Olive stops frequently to rest. At the end of the day a peak has still not been reached. The birds stop and are quiet in the trees above. Vines tangle across the path and the undergrowth is thick with ferns and saplings. Stepping off the track, Olive presses into the vegetation. Plants flatten beneath her body. She will sleep here. Taking the last orange from her pocket and a piece of chocolate she slowly eats.

Darkness drops and the night noises begin. Leaves rustle and a morepork calls. The soil is cold. Olive curls on her side. Her sleep is deep and without dreams.

Tuis warble in the trees at dawn. Olive sits up and rubs her eyes. Her hunger has gone and she is rested. Her arms and legs stretch effortlessly and she takes great breaths of clean air. Jumping to her feet she looks around. Yellow light filters down through the bush and those leaves in its way are translucent. The birds hop on the track ahead. Their wings splay open showing soft down and they are in the air. Bunched together, their flight is lazy. The wings rise and fall in slow motion as they glide forward. The green bird keeps to the centre. Silver feathers flash on either side.

Stepping forward, Olive follows them. The path dips down for a short time then continues upwards. The bush is denser here. Massive trees rise from the forest floor and the undergrowth on either side is barely penetrable. Her left shoe flaps and the sole splits away from the upper. Bending over, she takes both shoes off and her socks and leaves them on the path. Her feet are white and wrinkled. Long bones run the length of them. Strong feet, she thinks. They carry her forward.

In the middle of the morning the birds stop and rest in the branches overhead. Olive leans against a tree. Her back fits into a hollow in the wood and leaf mould cushions the ground. Patches of blue show through the foliage above. For a time she dozes then she is aware of the birds all around her and she is rising to her feet.

The journey continues on through the middle of the day. During the afternoon the path levels for the first time but the bush is too close to see anything.

There is some change in the birds' flight. A number of them leave the path and dart up into the trees. Their movements as they split and rejoin the group are lighter.

The path continues, neither rising nor falling, then a blaze of light appears ahead and the bush opens out. As the birds fly from the forest into the light they turn and their feathers are shot with gold.

Olive runs and she is out of the bush and in the clearing. She blinks in the sunlight. It is a mountain top. Far below, the land stretches in ridges and valleys and way out at its edge the sea is a blue-grey line. She cries out with pleasure. Taking off her damp coat and rolling up her trouser legs she stretches her limbs. The air is soft and the warm fragrance of sun on trees drifts up the hillside.

Turning, she looks out in the other direction. The bush thins out a long way below and paddocks and orchards chequer the land. Houses are tiny dots and windbreaks are darker lines of green. Near the horizon the city spreads and the sea is pale beyond. Hazy on the outer edge it merges with the sky. The birds soar up into the air and circle above the peak. The heavens stretch forever.

Olive is overwhelmed by the sight. She looks at the bush and the farms and the city and the sea and it seems there is everything to choose.

She stands poised on a jutting boulder at the edge of the mountain top and her arms are out. Then the warm bush-scented air flows up and her bare feet lift from the ground and she is in the air. A great laugh erupts from her belly and she floats up so the peak is below and the silver birds flash all around her. Tender wings touch her face and hands as they twirl above and below.

Olive tilts a little as she levitates. To the left, she thinks, and her body sideslips. The hair blows back off her face. Her back arches and she is pulling out of the dive.

'Ah ha!' she cries and the birds pass as lights in front of her eyes.

She glides on the air currents. The movements are effortless and her body is free and light. Her intention sets the direction. She is flying and the silver birds are flying with her. The peak shows jutting up from the range below and beyond that the lower land runs in folds and creases between the Pacific Ocean and the blue Tasman Sea.

Olive swoops and glides. Skimming to one side she rolls and planes back up. The sun is warm on her upturned face. She is alive. She laughs and laughs. It is her choice. Her shirt billows and cracks in the wind and looking down she sees that her trailing legs and arms are plump and pink.